Ruby

Ruby

Cynthia Tarr

Tuesdays Books,
an imprint of Cartwheel Bookends
Sonoma, CA

Published in the United States by Ruby Books, an imprint of Cartwheel Bookends, Sonoma, California.

First Edition

ISBN 978-1-7348483-0-4

Cover painting and design by: David Barker

Author photo by: Curtis Tarr

Visit Ruby's website:

www.TuesdaysBooks.com

For those who don't believe, no explanation is possible. For those who do believe, no explanation is necessary.

For Cliff - you have answered dreams
I never even knew I had

For Byron - my eternal Riley. I miss
you every day, buddy

And to Shivers - my Sam. Ruby
wouldn't exist without you

1

"STARRY, STARRY NIGHTS..." Ruby sang quietly, in a low, luscious, breathy voice. She sang as she sat out on the roof of her house, visually taking in that big gorgeous Midwestern sky. Her hand unconsciously reached back halfway into the roof opening to touch and pet her beloved dog, Mutt.

"Starry, starry nights." She exhaled, then stopped.

"What a beautiful night!" she mused, out loud.

"And what a stupid, fucking song."

One out of two ain't bad, she thought, reasoning it out. She could and did appreciate her life now, but she couldn't completely let go of her cynicism. It had to be housed in her brain, along with a constant music loop going at all times. Though there weren't a lot of chances for her to sing out loud at present, that didn't stop the music from coming.

And what a tawdry little mental/musical procession that could be! There was no quality control on the songs that would play inside Ruby's head, usually leaning heavily on whatever she had heard most recently. If, for instance, the last song she heard was a commercial for Love's Diapers, then all day long, till the next song was able to abscond with her mental train, life would unfold before her accompanied internally by a bevy of ad singers, singing/whispering "Love's! Love's!"

Sometimes the music loops came in handy. More than a couple of times, Ruby had gotten stuck in a loop, only to hone in on the lyrics she was singing to herself and find that they contained the exact answer she needed right then. Hmm. Follow Your Lyric Intuition? Was there a self-help book in that?

But far more important than sorting through those musical loops was this moment. The chance to breathe in the spiritual transcendence afforded her each and every night here in her old, yet new, home of Wisconsin.

The old home part was never far from her mind. She grew up in Wisconsin. Not far from here at that, in the college town of Appleton.

Born to working class parents, Fred and Diane Barnett, the paint on the completed portrait of their marriage and family life had already dried well before Ruby arrived. They had the one token son and the one token daughter. The family for those four was, for all intents and purposes, complete.

Well later, Ruby showed up. Was she a mistake? She always thought so, although she knew her parents wouldn't have said that. They also wouldn't have reassured her that the opposite was true either. Their shared attitude was one of just kind of weathering the storm that was "her." A sudden extra mouth to feed was Ruby's first and most fundamental identity.

Of course, her parents never said that! They didn't have to. The whole family was clear on it from the beginning. The sheer fact of Ruby seemed to make her folks just pull their pants up higher and keep their noses to the grindstone. It was much the same as when one suddenly needed a new car. You just had to forego what you must to afford what was in front of you.

Ruby took it in stride. She, for one, was happy for the mistake that had resulted in her life.

Despite the family penchant for deep, furrowed brows, Ruby lived a rather carefree life. Her siblings were far ahead of her in age and worlds different in outlook. They had already resigned themselves to life being an endless chore. Her parents were resigned to their lot in life as well. It always seemed that they were just a little too tired to directly notice or care for one more child.

That meant Ruby was on her own. Early on, she got the

hang of this system and figured out how to call her own shots. She might not be seen or appreciated within the family but then again, she could constantly reinvent herself without direct recrimination or even all that much notice.

Making waves was Ruby's specialty. She was beautiful, even then, not self-conscious despite her great body and great acting and singing talents. Starring in the plays and singing in the shows all the way through school, she had a million friends. She sometimes mused that she could have had even more friends than she did—except for one little thing.

She didn't care.

Not in a sociopathic way or anything. She loved those that she loved, for the length of time she loved them. She cared about a lot of things. But she always had the sense that she was, more or less, just getting through this period of time till she could get into the real part of her life. She would never have been able to explain that to anyone, but she knew the challenges and high points in her life weren't to be lived out here or in high school.

In fact, from the very first day of high school, Ruby had an immediate sense that she knew how to win this smaller game— what to say, what to do, who to rub the right way. Perhaps because she had that sense, she also knew that the winning wasn't going to mean all that much.

Without putting her finger on it, Ruby knew that there were

future challenges that would shape her to her core. But that would be later. Not here and not now.

It was upon graduating, when she told her family that she was heading out to Hollywood, that she got the biggest rise out of them yet. Which still wasn't all that much.

The family's reactions ranged from irritated ("I guess she just doesn't get it") to resigned-resignation being their family crest ("What can we expect? We didn't even look at her report cards!").

The family didn't offer her any help in this endeavor and she didn't ask for any. Ruby had been working all the way through high school to raise enough money to get out of Dodge and get on with it.

Getting out had always been the plan.

2

HOLLYWOOD HANDED RUBY ALL the hard knocks that she could have anticipated—and then some.

Despite the massive influx of new faces arriving yearly to "Tinseltown," Ruby didn't get swept aside, or become completely invisible, like so many did right off. She enrolled in a good performing arts junior college called Los Angeles City College and did some good parts in a couple of shows while there.

It wasn't that people didn't know what Ruby had. In fact, her singing had continued to grow in power, range and texture, far beyond her high school voice. She was proud of that growth. She performed from time to time in clubs around town with musician friends to great reactions, as well as singing backup vocals and demos for artists and songwriters.

It didn't take too long for Ruby to realize that she was in the midst of a life-sized rude awakening. From high school—where things were sort of so simple that it wasn't even inspiring—to show business. And show business was no game. At least in the sense that you could win it. It was a game that had no rules and no road map.

If there was ever a quirky or creative way to win at the Hollywood game, a handful of people had won that way already and after they had, that loophole had closed up.

The business forced Ruby and everyone else in it to constantly be figuring out what made you beautiful, what made you talented, what made you special or even more importantly—what made you some producer's wet dream. This was additionally frustrating when you were one of a thousand beautiful, talented wet dreams out there. If you lost out, you never knew why. Hell, even if you booked something, you never knew why.

So Ruby and thousands of hopeful actors would audition and schmooze and go to meet people, all the while trying to be "special" and not really seeing a way to get there. It was agony— mentally, physically and emotionally.

Oh, and then one more little wrench would get thrown into the hearts and minds of these struggling actors. Just when it seemed that no one would be granted entrance into this exclusive world of performing—the world where you got paid to perform—the Universe would pluck one extra little broken heart string. Out of pure chance in this deep cesspool of thousands for any one job, someone would rise up and nab the brass ring getting one great job after another. This would leave everyone else in her wake, wondering. Why? She wasn't the prettiest or the most talented or the most special or the most anything!

It was impossible, Ruby finally realized. Every day, the newest and shiniest contestants would arrive in LA for the game, untainted, undaunted, full of what they deserved and ready to take on the world. They didn't know yet about the lack of rules or a path, so they were fresh and excited, sure that all you had to do was work hard.

"And another hundred people just got off of the train…" Stephen Sondheim's lyric would often pop up in Ruby's musical loop.

A wise teacher had once told her that one way to keep from losing was to keep the game going forever. Most people, including Ruby, stayed a few extra years in Hollywood on that strategy alone.

Hollywood was a talent and soul lottery, with very, very few winners and thousands left asking themselves what they did wrong, where they turned off and why they had come up short.

A soul-less place filled with soulful people, Ruby often thought. It was those soulful people that had kept her in that town-far longer than her hope had.

❧ ❧ ❧ ❧ ❧

During the years that Ruby had been in Los Angeles, both of her parents had died. They actually died within a year of each other. This wasn't entirely surprising, as both of them had inhaled a lot of toxic crap at their factory jobs as wire weavers. That environment, plus a complete lack of any kind of exercise on both of their parts, seemed to seal their fate even before Ruby had left town. They were older, they were tired and they weren't healthy. So there was little surprise when they passed.

Still, there was one little surprise. The surprise was that no one had even bothered to let Ruby know of their deaths or invite her to any type of ceremony. Maybe they thought she wouldn't come. Maybe her siblings didn't even have a ceremony for them or do anything all that big to commemorate their passing. That would seem to match the passion with which her family did most things. And the truth was, she realized, that by not asking, they had absolved her of having to figure out if she even wanted to go back.

❧ ❧ ❧ ❧ ❧

Ruby realized that she had played out her youthful strategy of staying above it all extremely successfully. So much so that, in all the years since she had left Wisconsin, she had never dealt with or even thought about the reality of being unloved, unseen, or unappreciated by her immediate family.

But that ignorance phase ended with a bang. The snub over the lack of invitations—or even notices—to these services brought up a steamer trunk full of psychological crud to be dealt with. There was only one choice. Off to therapy she went.

Working with Viola was a turning point. Viola was both metaphysical and no nonsense. She could either be loving to Ruby or she could bug the shit out of her. Ruby loved that. And hated it! And then loved it some more. Viola saw all of Ruby and dealt with all of her. That alone was revelatory.

With Viola's help, Ruby dredged up large vats of anger that had been hidden down inside, both about her life growing up and her time in Hollywood. She started intensely working out at a gym to clear up and deal with her anger and its accompanying emotions. She studied Krav Maga, the Israeli self-defense system, for several years with a great teacher named Yaron. Yaron saw both Ruby's personality and her potential. He taught her all the proper techniques to fight as well as all the dirty tricks. It was just the formula she wanted—anger released while her strength kept increasing. She literally worked her ass off.

It felt good to be fit and strong. She had never been averse to pushing herself hard. And unlike acting, with Krav Maga, the harder you worked, the further you got! The strength and long hours at the gym began to fill her back up. It also helped her to transcend the horrifying body image obsession that lurked in every corner of that crooked town. After training so hard in the ring that she couldn't breathe or talk, she finally discovered that she could trust herself.

Cleansing and evolving began. In therapy, Ruby encountered some devastating self-doubt. But at the same time, Viola helped her to discover which people were truly safe for her to be around and how to trust the right people to help her.

She knew that this self-doubt, a gift from her parents' neglect, would still pop up, but now when it did, she had two options. She could see it for what it was and either directly deal with it or tax herself physically till her sense of perspective came back and the doubt went away.

The years were moving by. Sensing that the dream of becoming a big star was already laughably behind her, she learned how to not blame herself for that. The sheer numbers of hopefuls involved in this acting racket now somehow enabled her to step back and "take the blame off Mame," an inner musical loop sung over and over internally in the shaky voice of Rita Hayworth.

Old movies were another reason that kept her here. She adored movies. Growing up, Appleton faithfully played the latest action movie or comedy each weekend, but it was in LA that she got schooled in film. At least once a week, she went by herself for cannelloni to the Cafe Fig and then off to the local arts theatre to catch up on all the wonderful films she had missed.

Like every other acting hopeful, Ruby had a ton of part-time jobs. She would start each job hoping to find a great family atmosphere or great working situation, hoping that a new job alone would make the years go by easier. But every one of them brought either immediate or eventual disappointment.

Reaching the end of her rope waiting tables and tending bar, she knew she could make 200+ drinks in two hours or carry four dinner plates with perfect balance, but these were skills she had honed while inwardly hoping she could forget them as soon as possible.

So Ruby became a certified clinical hypnotherapist. Never interested in hypnosis as a magic trick, she really loved the potential of the healing it promised. Interestingly, hypnosis started off as her practice but in a very short time, the word went out that she was first and foremost a counselor, occasionally using hypnosis, as well as many other types of healing modalities.

Once Ruby opened her practice, many clients came to

her. As they did and as she began to listen to their life stories, a subtle but important transition occurred. People had always been drawn to Ruby for the promise of her beauty and vibrancy, but now she was also drawn to them.

She had been to battle—the battle for one's soul as you seek your dreams—and she had survived it, humbled. But she was still terminally curious. Helping others began to balance her.

She was becoming complete.

It was during this period of seeing clients, working out, watching films and doing her work with Viola that another realization crept into her gut.

Ruby missed Wisconsin.

An intense love for the land of her youth had always run deep for her. As a child, whenever she felt lonely or confused or lost, she would run to a field nearby. She would lay down and look up at the stars, comforted by the silos in the distance, cows grazing...and eventually, she would be whole again.

That Midwestern land had, for so many years, been the deepest and most lovingly reciprocal relationship she had ever known.

The role that land had played and filled for her had been hiding out in the recesses of her brain; lost to her memory till now. At first, when she had found the way to leave Wisconsin and get to LA, she hadn't been in any hurry to go back. She then realized with Viola that, though no one had invited her back, she could have always gone anyway. But there could be nothing there for her while her immediate and distant family with their foreboding resignation still remained.

It was at the same time she was discovering all of these feelings about the land, that suddenly the rules and the whole backdrop of Wisconsin changed. Ruby found out her sister was going to move away.

Her brother had left long ago, before her parents died. He now lived an even more resigned little life in far off Missouri with his taciturn wife and ugly kids. But her sister, Sara, was still there. So the coast wasn't clear to go back yet.

Then came word, via formal announcement, that her sister's husband had gotten a promotion in his job with Caterpillar tractors. They were moving to the Twin Cities in Minnesota.

Ruby didn't write or respond to this card or its news. Since her sister hadn't included anything personal with it, she didn't write her anything personal back.

But now a new plan began to grow. It was a plan that felt at once new and somehow preordained as well.

The land of Wisconsin, her birthright, free of all family, beckoned to her. She could finally return to it.

3

———

WHEN RUBY LEFT LOS ANGELES to move back to Wisconsin, she left with very little. She made a deal with her friend Janice to ship the rest of her stuff if she decided to stay. She jumped in her old Honda that had so many miles on it that all she could do was pray that it would take her at least the whole way there before it collapsed.

She didn't really have much to take-just some clothes and a bunch of books. She had her tunes to play for moral support, ones that she loved as well as demos that she had recorded or had sung on. She also brought some whiskey, for physical support and sheer warmth, in case she had to stay in her car some night along the way.

There was only one more thing to put in the car and it was

her favorite thing in the world. It was her dog, Mutt. She had called him a mutt the first time she laid eyes on him at the shelter and he had immediately jumped up and licked her all over. The name and the friendship stuck. Numerous love songs would pop in Ruby's mind looking at Mutt and she would sing them all to him, his gaze at her unwavering.

Oh, but wait. There was one other thing she was bringing back with her. She was coming back with a different last name.

To understand her new last name, you wouldn't have to consult Ruby's marriage history. She didn't have any. But you would have to understand her drinking history.

Growing up in Wisconsin, everybody drank. It was cold a lot of the year, work was very physical and the living for most of the population was pretty hard. So they drank quietly, with resignation. Their drinking didn't surprise her. Ruby knew that she wanted to drink as much as they did, but she didn't want to be a hypocrite about it. She wanted to be able to drink gaily in public, like the grand dames of old film had done. And she wanted to be able to hold her liquor.

What good was slobbering quietly and then passing out? She had always planned on being a big drinker and a good one too. After all, she reasoned, she had as much to forget about as any of these other sods did!

So, like everything else she was interested in, Ruby made

drinking into a study. She drank prodigiously, as only someone in their 20's could. While she worked as a bartender, she got to study the different patterns of getting drunk. And, like most things she put her mind to, she got eerily good at it.

One day, Janice bet her that she couldn't get the secret of what the next play was going to be out of this stuck up guy, Dash, in the Drama Department at Los Angeles City College. He knew what it was going to be and everyone knew he knew it but he was holding on to it like the Shroud of Turin. The bet intrigued Ruby enough to say she'd do it.

It was very easy for her to glean if a guy was attracted to her and she knew this guy was. She also knew that he didn't deem her to be at his level in the department yet, so he was waiting to see how far up she'd go before he made his move.

She couldn't wait until her station improved and still win this bet so she walked up and asked him out for a drink. Dash couldn't turn that down so off they went.

She drank him under the table, got the answer she was looking for and then sweetly begged off, pleading an early class. From that moment on, she knew she had an important tool in her arsenal. The drinking thing was well under her control...

Oh, well. Except for this one night.

Out with some hard drinking friends of hers, she was partying fairly hard. She had sought them out to party, as she was trying to forget the suspense she was feeling over a possible role in a TV pilot that she was very close to landing. It could change everything.

Ruby could never remember, thinking back, how she found out, somewhere in that evening that she didn't get the role. But she found out. And that was it. She heard that news and was really and truly done. All bets were off. All limits were off, too.

The party kept on going. It lasted throughout the night and into the next day, employing some fairly good drugs as well, just to make it all the more interesting.

Anyway, it would seem that on that following day, at the appropriate office for this kind of thing, there had been a name change requested and given.

Ruby Barnett from Appleton, Wisconsin, was now Ruby Tuesday. Yep. You heard right.

Why this name for a woman who was not even a particular Stones fan and who had never once set foot in the restaurant chain of that name either? Ah well. Life moves on and she could always change it back. And yet it felt a little like a Marine getting a tattoo overseas that was as weird as it was strangely commemorative.

So that was it for the Hollywood chapter of her life.

Ruby Tuesday and her dog, Mutt, were off to reclaim the land of her youth. And, possibly, of their future.

4

———

THE MINUTE RUBY CROSSED back over the state line into Wisconsin, she was in love.

She felt strong! Strong in the feeling that everything she had gained in LA—in selfawareness, empathy, curiosity, lessons learned on the randomness of success, recognizing that failure was fleeting—could all pay off. She was a soldier who had stepped off the battlefield, but had stepped off with some skills. And some fierce battle-weary pride.

As she passed from the endless flat lands of Illinois into the rolling green hills of Wisconsin, it always seemed to her to be the clearest cut division between any two states in the union. From the endless and flat sight lines of the hours previous, one passed into Wisconsin's green majesty—its silos, its cattle, its cornfields, those fragile, almost fallen barns—haunted by their own histories and gorgeous in their frailties.

And those skies! Always displaying a panorama of big fluffy clouds! Oh, how she had missed this land!

Ruby had no idea what she was headed into, but she knew the love of this land that had nagged at her and that she was now feeling again was a fact. A fact that would never leave her again, no matter how or where the story ended.

Driving north, she passed through Madison, Wisconsin's capital city, a city that she had never really spent any time in but had heard was nice. Wait a minute, had she even heard that? No matter. In time, she would find out for herself.

Each city she passed through while heading north had its own lake meandering through it. Many of the little towns had fairly dried up main streets. It stirred up Ruby's "Last Picture Show" sense of romance as she imagined tumbleweeds rolling through these beautiful, neglected but somehow preserved little towns.

She saw the signs to go east to Milwaukee, a city that she had seen plenty of in her wilder high school days and loved, thank you very much. She would have to at least go back there before leaving, if she did leave. It was just too cool a city to ignore if you were even remotely near it.

She wasn't at all sure where she was headed, if she was being honest. She knew she didn't want to head directly to hometown territory. There would be time for that, but not right away.

The drive across country had begun to teach Ruby about herself and how she was coming across, in her post Hollywood life. It was true here in her home state as well. There was a new power that came off of her, even when she wasn't aware of it. Walking into coffee shops and bars, all heads turned. When she first spoke in these places, all ears listened.

Sure, some of this was the outsider thing. She already knew well that, in the Midwest, one could never just melt in as an outsider. Being an outsider was a thing to be dealt with, as anyone and everyone in the room would instantly make clear to you. You weren't automatically accepted into the main populace. You had to earn that acceptance. And that earning period could take a long time. As a teenager here, Ruby had always been nice to outsiders. She prayed some of her karma on that score might come back to her.

But there was more to be dealt with than just that. Ruby was definitely beautiful here. She was beautiful in LA, but so were a million other people. Hell, every single waitress in LA was gorgeous.

Her voice was low and self-assured. That stood out. She strode in, comfortable in her body, head held high. That stood out. She was a large presence but complete within herself. That stood out. She hadn't left the state with this body but she had it now, closer to perfect than she had ever hoped it would be. It was a good enough body for LA, but it was almost spooky good here. And yeah, that stood out too. Her whole package inspired reactions, which she was able to assess immediately, even if there were no expressions on faces.

She was driving through places now where people worked hard for their money. Many of them were overweight and very few of them bothered with their appearances. They had eventually lost concern for this level of things. Getting enough food on the table daily for their children took a higher priority.

Ruby understood them and as a culture, she knew them. She loved them. They were, though they had no idea of this as they stared openly at her, her people! She had grown up within them. But now, after all her years in LA, when she walked into a room there was a sea change. At the very least, she would be meeting them in a new way.

It was a comprehensive change. Unlike in LA, where your every attribute was sized up like a junk dealer who was only concerned with buying certain parts, Ruby began to see that she was a whole person to these people. An alien whole person to be sure, but a whole person just the same.

Perhaps she was truly and finally where she should be.

That thought alone made her burst out laughing in the middle of her chicken fried steak at the Wauwatosa Diner.

5

IF SHE WAS HONEST with herself, Ruby was always probably going to end up in Rural, at least for a little bit.

When she was young, her family had taken a few summer vacations to the Chain 'O Lakes in Waupaca, Wisconsin. One of her dad's buddies had a cottage on Round Lake. When this friend wasn't using his place there and no one above him on the food chain at work that could help his career wanted to use it in his absence, he would offer it to her dad for the family.

On initial visits, Ruby had stayed in the background, walking in the fields at night while her older siblings went to the bars. But later, when they had moved out, she would beg to go and grew to love those lakes. She even lost her virginity there on the ground near a canoe with the lake shimmering and the sounds of crickets and feel of the wind...

What a night! The sex hadn't been much to write home about but the production values were amazing!

There was a picturesque and tiny town near those lakes called Rural. The main reason the kids knew about Rural at all was because it was where you put your inner tubes in the water to start floating down the Crystal River rapids.

The Crystal River wound through Rural and out again.

For as long as Ruby could remember, Rural had shown up in her dreams. There was some kind of unfinished business for her there. She had fleeting thoughts about it when her family was still all in place. But now, with everybody gone, Rural was pulling her in, irresistibly.

They reached Rural and stopped right in the tiny center of it. Even Mutt, who Ruby knew could find magic anywhere, jumped out of the car, barked, ran around in a little circle, stopped in his tracks and wagged his tail as he looked up at Ruby.

"I know, Mutt. Me too," she told him. "I don't know how or why. But we were meant to be here. Haven't the first clue how to make this work but..."

Mutt barked again and kept looking right at her.

"Me too, buddy," she repeated, as they stared at each other.

6

WITHOUT A LOT TO explore in Rural, Ruby went into the little general store for clues, as well as to pick up some dog food for Mutt.

The inside of the store was teeny tiny. It was most likely dwarfed by the full size Piggly Wiggly, only minutes away in Waupaca. Ruby had seen the signs for it. But suddenly, in the small slice that was Rural, it seemed to Ruby to be exactly the right size.

She had to adjust her eyes to the darkness as she walked inside. A couple was inside running it, if you could call it that. Mostly it seemed like they walked around silently, passing each other without speaking.

Ruby found the dog food and put it on the counter to let

them know she was going to be buying something. It seemed pretty old, so she just got one can and made a mental note to visit the Piggly Wiggly in town. All romance aside with the general store, Mutt was worth it.

"Is it okay if he comes inside with me? He won't hurt anything," she asked, to no one in particular. The couple looked at each other and the wife nodded. She then disappeared in back for a bit and came out with a water dish that she put on the floor in front of Mutt.

"Oh, thank you so much!" Ruby over gushed, getting no real response in return. The woman had done a nice thing for her dog but she obviously didn't want Ruby to think it bonded them in even the smallest of ways. Ruby reminded herself once again that this was the Midwest and you had to earn your inclusion.

The store had a tiny bit of everything. It was obvious that most people came in here for souvenirs, so about half of the store consisted of unrelated knick knacks. She roamed around, looking at the old vinyl records and funny refrigerator magnets, taking time to see the whole store. She didn't really know where she was going after this, so there didn't seem to be a big hurry to leave. Mutt was happy just to sniff new dust and smells.

Ruby was having a hard time squelching the doubt that was beginning to creep into the edges of her consciousness and make its way toward mental center stage. What have I done?

she wondered. LA wasn't great and it was definitely time to leave, but...here?

She didn't even have a place to stay and here she was, following some romantic dream that had no logic or grounding behind it. Would her parents have thought she was daft to come back? Should she leave? But where to go? And why had she been so sure that she should start here?

There was a nest egg left for her, from her parent's estate, that she had planned to use once here as a down payment or at least rent for a year till she got her bearings. She had received the notice about it but she had been adamant about not touching it for several years, knowing it was her ticket out of LA. Now she knew it was time to use it. But here? Really?

It had truly seemed like she was being pulled here, as if by a ridiculously strong magnet. These directed or pulling feelings had begun to pop up a lot lately. Almost like she was being specifically guided. She followed them when they came up, partially because they seemed so tangible and partially because she felt lost enough at sea that "any port in a storm" seemed to carry the day.

She and Mutt were in the store's tiny back room browsing when she heard a voice up front. It was an older man's voice, soft spoken. He greeted the couple as old friends did. They all spoke quietly but with a definite knowledge of one another. There was the sound of several things being placed on the counter.

"So, three cans of soup then, Frank?" the shop man asked. "Is that going to be enough?"

"More than enough," the man said quietly. "In fact, I don't need that many. Let's take one out."

There was the sound of the one can being taken out and then being put back in the group by the shop man. "You can put it on your tab, you know."

Ruby was now peering through a display case at the scene. She saw a good looking older man. He was quite thin, but still had a regal stance about him. His life seemed a bit downtrodden, yet he still had an air of class and bearing.

"No. No more of that, Roger. My tab is too big already and completely unpayable. You and I both know that. Just the two soups."

"But Frank...," the shop man said with more emotion that Ruby had imagined she would see out of him.

Frank was weary and couldn't argue any more. "Please, Roger. If you have a bag, it is a long walk." And with that, he shuffled out the door.

It was clear that this man was much further down on his luck that she initially would have guessed. But he walked out and deliberately headed down the road, crossing the Crystal River Bridge on his way home.

Next move is yours, Ruby thought. Or did she actually not think it but hear it? At this point, she still didn't know but also didn't feel willing to question.

She waited until he was far enough away. Then she grabbed a couple of soup cans and put them on the counter with the dog food can. Thinking fast, she also grabbed some saltines. The shop man rang them up. It was clear that he knew what she was doing and it was also clear that he didn't think it would work. All of this was clear with no talking.

As she paid, he finally spoke. "Three miles down after the bridge. Good luck. I've tried but...," he trailed off.

"It can't hurt to try. But just in case I fail, could you take this for his account?" she said, handing him a twenty.

He smiled for the first time. Not a big smile. In fact, it would have been easy to miss. But Ruby was looking for it.

She and Mutt sat in the car, watching the man as he got smaller on the horizon. When she was sure he was getting to his destination, she started the car. She wasn't entirely sure what she would find. Was he in a shack or something? Who cared. This was clearly the next step, wherever it would lead.

She drove slowly, but not stalker slowly. Her luck went up a tick as he turned into his driveway, making her timing work just right.

She was surprised to see him moving towards a beautiful little home with a waterwheel next to it, dried up but still pretty with the top of a barn sticking up in back. As she continued to inspect it more closely, there was plenty to do to get this place back on its feet. In fact, the top of the barn looked like it might be leaning...

He heard her pull in and turned. She knew she had to stop and get out quickly so he couldn't turn her away.

"Stay here for now, Mutt, and keep your paws crossed."

Mutt promptly sat down and crossed his paws. It was a trick that she had taught him for luck when she was waiting to hear about parts and singing gigs. She didn't always get them when he did that, but his trick would always charm her all the same. Maybe it could work this time?

"Pardon me," she spoke out quickly to the man. "I know I'm doubtless intruding here, but I was in the store back there when you were and you got soup. It made me so nostalgic for the bean with bacon soup I had as a child. I used to live near here and we always had it with saltines and I haven't had it since. I bought some but I don't have anywhere to cook it. Would it be possible for me to come in and eat my soup with you, or you could have some too, or I could pay you for the use of your stove?" She knew she had gone too far but had to get all the options out there.

He looked at her dubiously but not unkindly. There followed a Midwestern silent moment. It was long and she knew she had to wait for his decision. Oddly, she could feel the sense growing in her mind that his decision was somehow incredibly important to her, to him and to their future.

Finally, he appeared to give in. He laughed a quiet laugh and shrugged. "Well young lady, it takes all kinds. Lucky for you, I'm free this afternoon. So why not?"

As she followed him, she asked, "It's okay if the answer is no, but would you be alright if I brought my dog Mutt in? He won't disturb anything."

He stopped, turned and nodded. She went back and opened the car. Mutt bounded out, ran to the man and stopped, hoping to be petted by this new human.

Tears sprang to the old man's eyes as he reached down and petted the dog. His gnarled hands seemed sure and familiar as he touched Mutt.

"Great dog," he said with a smile. "What's his name?"

"Mutt."

He snorted. "That's the best you could come up with?"

"Nah, but it stuck. Every time I tried something cuter, he didn't answer to it. So he's Mutt."

"Well, welcome to my home, Mutt."

As he and Mutt walked forward with Ruby in tow, she knew

that the love affair between Mutt and Frank had just started. She was going to be relegated to excess baggage for the time being.

Fine with me, she muttered to herself.

1

———

THE INSIDE OF FRANK'S HOUSE resembled the outside—once very sweet and looked after, now hopelessly neglected.

Ruby realized her most difficult obstacle while in this house was the dust everywhere with her allergies. She quickly popped an allergy pill from her pocket and just hoped she wouldn't start sneezing continuously.

Ruby's job growing up while her parents worked was to clean the house. She complained about it, so they would know how hard it was on her to do the whole house. But in truth, somewhere in the middle of all that cleaning, she had fallen in love with the practice. It was no real effort at all and was certainly the chore she would have chosen above all others. Her parents didn't mind or try to give her other chores, perhaps sensing out of sheer fatigue that if she didn't do it, it wouldn't get done.

She had even cleaned other student's apartments for rent money in LA. As long as they weren't gross, she put on her rubber gloves and went to work.

Ruby was getting itchy after just moments inside—partly from allergies and partly because she suddenly wanted to get in and clean this place. It wasn't really gross, after all. Just a little dusting alone could...Woah. Slow your roll, girlfriend, she said to herself.

"What a cool house!" she said earnestly, meaning it.

"I love it, too," he said quietly, with feeling.

Over two bowls of bean with bacon soup, they talked. Ruby gently prodded Frank to learn more about him. When she thought this private man had given up about as much information about himself as he would, she had an idea.

"Hey!" she almost shouted in this quiet house.

"You know what doesn't go with this at all but I want it anyway? I've got some whiskey in the trunk of my car. Do you go for that sort of thing?"

"Used to," he said with a small smile. "I wouldn't mind if you want to. But don't you have somewhere you should be getting to?"

"Yep," she said, looking right at him with confidence, "and I have finally gotten here."

8

___

OVER HIS FIRST SIPS of whiskey in quite a while, Frank told Ruby his story. He had lived in that house for forty years with his wife, Clara. Whenever he spoke of her, it wasn't with yearning. It was with a relaxation, as if reimagining her here just put things right.

Frank had been a teacher and the lay minister at his local church. Clara had helped a friend with an antique shop in Waupaca. Both Frank and Clara had wanted kids but couldn't have them. So he satisfied himself by helping the kids he worked with. Most of them were long gone now, but some still sent him a postcard from time to time. Ruby could tell that he had saved them and re-read them many times.

When he retired, he knew they couldn't really afford the house anymore. He suggested that they sell it and move into an apartment in Appleton. But Clara was frantic at the thought. This was the only home she had ever really known and she wanted to die there.

And die there she did. But by that time, the house was run down, way past the level where they could sell it, and the taxes were ten years past due. Frank's tiny retirement was just enough to keep the lights on, but not much else.

Ruby asked quiet questions and listened, honored that he would tell her all of this. He too seemed shocked by his candidness with her. But once it started, there was a sense of an acute need to tell it all, to get every bit of it out there. The fact that she was a stranger made her seem to be the ideal person for him to talk to.

Seeing what was coming, Ruby knew he was getting to the sad and hopeless part. She was feeling a little hopeless, too. She wanted this house badly—that much was clear to her. She wanted it the moment she turned into the driveway. But not at the expense of this lovely, quiet man.

To break things up, she said, with a little forced jocularity, "Hey Frank, I need to stand after drinking all this hooch. Do you think you might show me around a bit?"

They walked through the house. She wasn't able to walk into some of the rooms due to the dust and neglect. He didn't show her the bedroom he stayed in due to embarrassment, she figured. But everything about it was charming, or could be again.

She badly wanted to restore the love that Clara had invested in it. She knew that would not be all that hard. But could she live there with Frank? She liked him but knew that would be out of the question for both of them.

After the house, they looked at the dry waterwheel and Frank had fun recounting the building of it when they first moved in. He told her it still moved a little in the winter when it snowed but it groaned about it the whole time. They had their first laugh over that.

Then there was the barn she had glimpsed earlier over the roof. Close up, it was either leaning or she was leaning looking at it. Definitely past being a mere fixer upper. There was also a large field in the back where Frank said that he and Clara had once grown enough corn and vegetables to last them all year, with canning. Now the ground lay bare.

With just one exception.

She peered out and saw a dilapidated building at the end of the field. She mentioned it and they walked toward it. He told her he was embarrassed about it. It was where Clara had canned vegetables and worked on her garden projects. He hadn't opened the door to it in over ten years. They had to pry it open together.

Inside, it could scarcely have been more ramshackled. There was even a tree from outside that was growing into it, with roots coming through the floor. But there was plumbing and a bathroom. A bolt of lightning shot through her. In that second, the plan was now in place.

"Okay, Frank, I have an offer for you. Let's go back to the house and drink on it." They walked a little faster back to the house, both sensing that their lives were about to change.

An hour later, the plan was conceived and agreed on.

Ruby would begin to pay up Frank's old taxes. Rather than going into foreclosure, she would buy the house from him with a $10,000 payment and small monthly payments after that. She would pay for utilities and food. When he objected to that, she convinced him that food cost about the same amount for two as it did for one.

He would stay in the house with her while they rebuilt the house at the end of the field. She didn't know anything about building, but he did. After all, he had built that little back house decades ago! And she would help him. When he felt ready, he could move back there. They would work on the tiny house first and then eventually attack that barn.

"Here is the problem with your thinking," he said quietly, unwilling to get his hopes up. "I can't help you with any of the rebuilding. I don't have the physical ability any more to do any of it."

"But you know what should be done to fix everything?" she asked.

"Well sure. I made it work the first time...I know what has to be done, but."

"Then you are now the foreman of this project, Frank. I'll get help from someone else. Not to worry, you'll be worth your weight in bean with bacon soup for the duration."

"Come to think of it, there is a neighbor's kid who is pretty strong. He is a swimmer and whenever they have to go to regional meets, he walks around and asks if anyone needs some help, to raise money. I've never been able to hire him."

"There you go!" she answered quickly, not sure a swimmer would be the right way to go, but not wanting to break up the old man's hope and the tiny fire that was just starting to come back into his eyes. "We'll just be two day laborers, me and the swimmer guy, tools at the ready and awaiting your instructions!"

They drank and began to muse over ideas. After a while, she knew she had to voice her one big worry. "Frank, I know I can be happy here. Mutt is already happy here. But can you be happy living out back when this house has really always been yours?" She knew he would be honest with her, so she held her breath and waited.

As she would learn with Frank, there was always a pause before he spoke.

"My dear young friend, up until a couple of hours ago, I was looking at the prospect of being kicked off of this property. To stay on it, help to restore it and live on it in peace? You are the answer to a dream. And a prayer I had long since stopped praying. Thank you."

She gave him a moment and then spoke.

"That prayer goes both ways, Frank. We can do this." They didn't know how to seal the deal. They hadn't known each other long enough to hug, so they shook hands, looking with deep gratitude into each other's eyes.

And the world, slowly, began to turn again.

9

_____

AND WORK SHE DID. First she had to clean the big house. This work, Ruby knew how to do solo. She always had. So she shooed Frank out the door on walks with Mutt, telling him that Mutt needed to get the lay of the land. Which was true, but she also had another motive. She wanted Frank to get healthier.

Her fondness for him grew by the hour and part of restoring the house was going to be restoring him! She loved him already like the father she had always wanted. She wanted him to be around for years to come. But it was too soon to tell him that, so she kept it under wraps. Timing in relationships in the Midwest wasn't made; it was earned. Ruby could respect that.

Frank liked Ruby and more than that for now, he was grateful to her. He was right there, hands on, with the title transferring and the lien lifting. She imagined that there must have been a thousand moments of humiliation in the process for Frank, but he didn't show them to her. She could tell that he had made up his mind that she didn't deserve to be brought down by his emotions in this thing, so he did not share them. She knew Frank imagined that he had to privately navigate his path and his thoughts. But it wasn't really necessary, due to something he didn't know.

Ruby already knew his thoughts.

For as long as she could remember, Ruby could feel the psychic waves that passed between people. It was as if she could instantly gain an overview of someone and know them—their motives, whether or not they could be trusted, stuff like that.

Part of her success in high school stemmed from this gift. She could almost immediately read and see people, intricately and clearly. From this overview of clarity, she could sometimes see where someone was headed in life. She could already see them down the road.

This wasn't to say that Ruby was entirely free of wrong turns. She wasn't. There were a couple of bad boys back there that...Whew! Talk about your wrong turns. She must not have seen them coming.

But as time went on, she began to realize that those wrong turns had happened as a result of one of two things: Number

1—that either the guy was sexy and she really felt like getting laid, if you must know; or Number 2—for whatever reason, when said bad boy walked in, she had turned her gift of being able to read him off.

She read women quite well. She read men even better.

Ruby's looks and sexuality had always been a lightning rod to men. So reading them was a cinch. First off, it was easier to read men when they were coming at you, their dialogue laced with desire. And secondly, if their "rods" were currently involved in a hormonal electrical storm, they were absurdly easy to read. In seconds, she knew who they were now and what they would be like after "the lightning round" as it were.

There was no sexuality between Frank and Ruby, however far fetched it might have been if there was. But it wasn't there from the first minute. Ruby immediately chalked that one up in the plus column. She knew that sexuality, even when not acted upon, would always stay in the room. In this case, though, their room was clear of it.

She watched Frank move from sadness at losing the house, to gratefulness to her for saving the day, to genuine joy at getting to know her, and to delight at seeing the house springing back to life.

Ruby made a promise to herself, with regards to the house, that she wouldn't fundamentally change the vision that Clara had thought up and brought into this place, or at the very least, not until Frank wasn't here anymore. And even then, she doubted she would change it much.

Truth was, she liked Clara's energy here, an energy that began to be reanimated as she shined the house up again for her. Clara was there. She could feel more of Clara's love for the place as she uncovered more and more to love.

10

_____

RUBY WAS ENJOYING the work of fixing up the house. She had always loved a night where you could fall down on the sofa, exhausted, and know that you had honestly and truly earned that exhaustion.

Even though she had sent for her things and had set up her weights in the barn (the sturdiest corner of the barn, anyway), the aches she was feeling had nothing to do with the muscles she had worked so hard to develop in LA. Those were easy! No, now she had the additional ache of using muscles she never even knew she had!

Reality was dawning slowly on Ruby. She still had a nest egg but it wasn't getting any bigger. No one was paying her for the services she was providing to this house and she needed to be paid for some kind of services!

Her thoughts ran in two directions. She could see if there was any way she could start up her therapy practice again. But how could she do it without risking even weirder assessments from her new community? Every time she weighed it, it seemed like starting up her practice might be a long ways away.

The other idea and the more immediate one was just to find some place to work part time. Besides, she was getting close to needing to hire Flipper. That was her inner nickname for whoever that little neighborhood swimmer guy was. He was going to have to be paid for his help. While his sight and talents were still unseen, she still knew she needed help on some of the larger stuff, so she made a mental note that she needed some "Flipper" money to be coming in as well from somewhere.

Clearly, it was time for a job.

"No time like the present," she said to herself one morning upon waking up. She had noticed that she was less sore than the morning before, immediately prompting her to want to take a long walk. She would walk and, God willing, come home with a job. A long shot, to be sure, but stranger things had happened. I mean, look where she was now!

II

RUBY NEEDED SOME SUPPLIES in Waupaca and it was only a couple of miles there and back. She washed her face, shoved a book in her purse, swallowed her allergy meds, put on her dark glasses and set out.

As the heat instantly engulfed her, she found herself pining away for some marijuana. Man oh man! A little pot would have slowly sanded off the edges of this intense heat until she could feel complete acceptance.

Ruby loved some pot and had run out of her stash way too long ago, in a little motel in St. Louis. That was definitely a connection she needed to make. Ah well, she was headed to Milwaukee this weekend to meet up with the friend of a friend. Maybe that would yield something.

She walked through Waupaca. Even without the benefit of being stoned, she tried to zen herself into accepting the energy of what it would be like to work at each of these places.

Bridal wear? Wow. That would be tough. Grocery store? She could be a checker but it was still summertime and it seemed like everybody working there was in high school. Tough hours, too. She made a mental note to check back there when school was back in session if she still needed something.

The town bar? She peeked inside. Hmm. She knew she was a great bartender, which wouldn't even come into play in this little joint from the looks of it. She made a mental note to keep this one in play. They didn't look like they were hiring but everybody in the bar was male, including the bartender, so that boded well for her chances.

Two crafty hobby-like stores with two women in each of them. In both places the women were sour and stood there motionless and talking to each other, covering an array of brain dead subjects. Ruby knew immediately that the energy was all wrong. I would rather rake out stalls or do farm chores than shoot the shit with these two Mensa candidates, she thought to herself.

She told herself not to get down. It could work out anywhere if it had to. She kept telling herself that on the way to Wisconsin and she was still standing by it. She could make it work.

After all, on the plus side, this was only the first day looking for a job. Of course, on the minus side, she had already covered half the town.

Maybe there was a charming spot and job in a nearby town that wasn't too far of a commute away. Of course, she would have to get a newer car if that was the case. Her Honda, after getting her to Rural, was more than ready to be put out into car pasture.

Okay, no more thinking about this, she concluded. She headed down a side street to a little cafe she had read about in the local paper. Once there, she discovered that it was also a B&B called Lilac's Breath. She had burst out laughing at the weirdness of the name the first time she had seen it in the paper and seeing the sign in person made her laugh again. She waited until she could enter with a straight face.

The interior was strewn with lace and flower prints everywhere. It was so home spun, it was more like home strangled. She made her way into the small dining area where each table had a glass top that covered fabric with more lace and more flowers. She was grateful, at least, for the glass respite.

The proprietor's name was Dot. She was a large woman in a flower print sweatshirt with a big smile, a big voice and an extremely gregarious nature.

Once she spotted Ruby, she swooned over to the table, handing her a menu.

"Oh how lovely to see you! I don't think we've met, have we?"

"Nope, I don't think so."

"My name is Dot. That's what everyone calls me. Well, that's if they call me! Get it?" she howled, slapping Ruby on the shoulder in her mirth. "You can call me Dot. You can call me anything! Just call me!" Richard Pryor couldn't have made this woman laugh more than she could make herself laugh.

Now, Ruby could appreciate enjoying one's own company. She always had. But to work here would be to live inside of Dot's energy. It just took up the whole place. And Ruby felt too quiet for that, at least lately.

Her home life these days had very little noise and she liked that. A lot. She and Frank could eat dinner and never say a word for long periods of time. They talked too, but it simply wasn't necessary when it wasn't. They even played cards without talking. It felt like a spiritual retreat or something.

Scratching this off as a potential place of employment, she came back into the moment to notice that Dot was still talking. Whenever she asked Ruby a question and Ruby didn't answer, she just went right on. Quite obviously Dot had a lot of practice making that leap.

"What's good today, Dot? Quiche?"

"Oh, my goodness, yes. Let me see if there are one or two

pieces left...." The mention of two pieces made Ruby's heart sink, thinking she might be stuck with Dot as a dining companion. So she reached in her bag, once alone, and brought out her book, engrossing herself in it with all the dedication she could muster.

The quiche was indeed quite good with fresh vegetables in it. The light salad dressing was delicious. It was clear that Dot knew what she doing in the kitchen. Ruby resolved to think of her kitchen skills the next time Dot trapped her in conversation.

The meal had cheered her up—so much so that she splurged for dessert.

"How about a slice of your lemon mousse pie?" she asked Dot, who looked excited for her to try it. When it came, she bit into it.

Tasting the pie was a religious experience.

It was beyond good. It was soulful. Every bite had mystery and satisfaction in it.

Ruby could feel Dot's energy in the rest of the food, but not in this pie. But she had to ask, because if Dot made something with this much depth to it, there was more to Dot than she'd bargained for. So she did the thing that she knew would make Dot the happiest. She caught her eye and asked her over to the table.

"Good?" Dot asked, looking like she was going to jump for joy.

"Dot, it was way more than good. I have had a lifelong affair with baking and desserts and this is one of the best I've ever had."

"Oh, she'll love to hear that. Well, she hears it all the time. But you can never get tired of compliments, can you?"

"I should say not!" Ruby agreed, mirroring Dot's bubbly enthusiasm with her own. She knew she had to achieve just the right rapport to ask the next question.

"I hope this isn't a terrible thing to ask, but who made this pie? I'm not from around here and wonder whether some of my chef friends in Milwaukee would know of her. You are so amazingly smart to use her for your desserts!"

"Well, it isn't considered good business but oh well. I'll tell you anyway. My friend Cheryl always says, just ask Dot anything, she'll up and tell you! Ha! And I can pretty much guarantee that none of your Milwaukee cooks knows anything about her. She is our best kept secret!"

"And her name is…?" Ruby gently got Dot back on track.

"Reardon Passels, of course! Did you pass a donut shop on your way in here? Oh, I can see on your face you didn't. It is about a mile out, on the freeway. Anyway, that's hers. If you go by there, tell her Dot sent you. Uh-oh. Better not! Ha!"

As the hilarity, table of one, ensued, Ruby paid and slipped out. She was single-mindedly headed to a donut shop off the highway.

12

SINCE THE DONUT SHOP was going a mile in the wrong direction, Ruby had increased her total walk by two miles. But there was no way she wasn't going there right away. She could pick up groceries for dinner on the way back. Maybe she would even stop at Turner's Market and get some fresh corn, too. But first, the donut shop.

Ruby had no idea what she would encounter at this donut shop. But her Spidey sense was tingling, that was for sure. She saw it in the distance and was already coming up with a plan for buying a bike for the commute. Yep, she could cut off some time with a bike. Get here in twenty minutes, easy.

Once she reached Reardon's, it seemed almost closed down. It seemed to intentionally not draw attention to itself. Maybe a bad sign, she thought. Or possibly a really good sign.

Inside, the energy took a dramatic up sweep. The first thing Ruby noticed was that the place was immaculate. She had never seen a donut store that was this clean. For anyone in the know, that seemed to automatically promise great things.

There was a sweet young girl tidying up. Ruby put her age in high school, yet nothing like the checkout girls at the Piggly Wiggly. Her friendliness was polite and she seemed to know about the world beyond her. Or at least she knew that there was a world beyond her. A little perspective is a great thing to have, Ruby thought.

"Can I get you something?" she asked Ruby.

Ruby, reading her nameplate, said, "Yes. Trudy, is it?"

When the girl nodded, Ruby asked. "I've been walking quite a ways to get here, so two diet cokes if you have them?"

"Coming right up!"

"Oh, and Trudy, is Reardon...?"

"My mom."

"Is she around? I'd like to meet her."

"She's making a delivery, but she should be back here in about five to ten minutes."

After about eight minutes, two diet Cokes and a glazed donut worthy of high acclaim around this or any world, Reardon came in through the back door. Her daughter went to get her.

13

———

WHEN REARDON WALKED THROUGH the bakery door and into the restaurant, Ruby felt bathed in gentleness and greatness. This was a quiet woman, like Frank was a quiet man, but Reardon's quietude came from a whole different place. She was a master at something. No ifs, ands or buts about it. She could bake in any kitchen in the world and she knew it. But this seemed to release any ego from her. She wasn't searching for herself. She knew herself plainly, inside and out. Her brilliance and her foibles were both to be shrugged off. Life was life and she had her place in it.

When they introduced themselves, Reardon shrugged off her daughter's offer of a drink. She stood and got herself a lemonade. It was her store and yet she didn't take advantage of her daughter. Ruby noted and loved that. No need to exert power. And in the same way, she sensed that if Reardon really wanted or needed help, Trudy would have moved heaven and earth to get there.

Trudy seemed to get that Ruby wanted to talk to her mother, so she wisely left them to themselves. Ruby started right off describing eating the lemon pie, coming here and eating the glazed donut. She sensed that Reardon didn't seem to take to platitudes, so instead she described what this baking had felt like to her.

She seemed to have passed some quiet test because Reardon began to ask her more about herself. Ruby found herself sharing the whole story of coming here, the house, Frank, Mutt, even Dot.

Ruby leaned back, finished and shocked to have told that much, but Reardon kept looking at her. She asked a question.

"What are you going to do for work?" she asked directly, but without force. Force was not in this woman's deck.

"I...," Ruby was speechless.

"Well, you came here. Do you want a job working with me?"

"Would I?! Do you have a job for me? I mean, I don't want to displace Trudy."

Reardon smiled. "Don't worry. You can't displace her. She's my daughter. She comes with the territory."

Ruby felt ashamed that she had jumped to the conclusion that she was so "all that" that she would have pushed the woman's daughter out. Reardon pretended not to notice her blushing and simply went on.

"Here's the thing. You seem nice and you seem able. I could be wrong about that, but it doesn't happen too often. I do everything here myself. I work ten hours a day—from four to two o'clock. I do all my baking, then wait on customers for morning pick ups here, and then I do my deliveries to the restaurants. Trudy comes in after school to wait on people while I finish deliveries.

I've done this for years and I wouldn't mind someone helping me. I can hire you for four hours of each of those ten. You pick which ones. You can help me bake or you can help me deliver. I don't care which. Sound like something you might want?"

"But I have to tell you that my car..."

"You already told me that."

"I did?" Ruby couldn't believe how much she had told this woman!

"I have a truck and a Vespa here. You can drive either, as long as you have a valid license and you don't wreck them."

"That certainly seems more than fair."

"Good. This will help me. Glad you came along, Ruby. Oh. What is your last name anyway?"

"Tuesday."

"For real? Wow. Didn't see that coming."

14

RUBY WAS EBULLIENT GOING home that night. She knew that the money wouldn't be much, but far more to the point, she had found someone she could learn from, someone whom she felt completely safe with. And if that wasn't enough—and it was—she had located in a funny little shed-like restaurant off the side of the road...a master practicing.

Reardon was a woman who could bake anything. That much Ruby was sure of. She was also a woman who wanted for nothing outside of this moment. A woman comfortable in her own skin. What a blessing.

She also knew that she had a thing or two to offer back to Reardon. They both had known that. Reardon was not aware that Ruby knew a secret about her. She picked it up right away.

Now wouldn't be the time to talk about it, but sometime it would surely come up. And Ruby felt well equipped to help her with it.

She sang songs into the wind as she walked along the road toward home. No one could have heard her with that wind, so she sang as big as she felt like singing. What a lovely blessing to be singing again!

As she passed through Waupaca, she stopped for groceries. She felt like celebrating, so she got two steaks and baked potatoes for dinner. Frank would protest the price by saying instead that steak wasn't good for him, but she knew he would secretly be thrilled and would love to celebrate with her.

Lost in thought, she was in the grocery line waiting to be checked out when she looked up and noticed the checker's red swollen eyes. There was no one behind Ruby in line and it didn't look like anyone was coming, so she waited until the checker totaled her out and bagged her stuff before questioning her.

Reading her nameplate, Ruby said, "Stace? Are you okay?"

The question alone brought more tears to Stace's eyes. Not knowing Ruby, but not knowing where else to turn, Stace said, "No. I'm not. I'm not okay at all."

Ruby moved forward gently, touching her left elbow in an almost courteous gesture, letting her know she cared but not getting too close. Not touching her would have been the best choice, but Ruby instinctively knew that she somehow had to reach over the counter that was between them.

"Do you think it would be okay if you took five minutes off?" Ruby asked her, never leaving her eyes. Stace looked up at her manager, held up five fingers and pointed outside. The manager nodded and they walked out.

Once outside, Ruby stepped a safe distance away from Stace but made sure she was entirely visible under the light.

"Stace, you don't know me and you don't know that I'm trustworthy. But I am. I hold a lot of people's secrets in my head and I have helped a lot of people who came to me with eyes that looked just like yours."

At this, they both laughed a bit.

"I must look really terrible," she laughed and said, ruefully.

"Not terrible, but not your best, I'm guessing," Ruby said, keeping it light. "Your mascara bit the dust a while back." They both laughed a bit again.

"So I'm right here ready to listen, Stace. Take a chance and tell me what's going on."

With that, Stace haltingly launched into her fiance breaking up with her. The break up was very new and her emotions were right on the surface, while her ability to reason through the story wasn't there at all.

When Stace was at the end of her story, Ruby spoke. She told her a few things that made her think. As they spoke, she could tell that Stace was starting to look at her differently. Finally she had to ask.

"Who are you and how do you know all of this stuff?" she said, peering at Ruby with confusion but behind that, the beginnings of hope.

"I can tell you this. My name is Ruby. I'm new here but where I came from, I helped people to get through what you're going through. We can meet up and I can help you if you want." She took out a pen from her bag and wrote her name and phone number on Stace's palm. "First meeting is on me."

Stace looked hopeful but had to be sure.

"You say you helped people who were as bad off as me?"

"I helped people much worse off."

"And are they okay now?"

Ruby thought with love about some of her old clients.

"They are thriving," she said, smiling. And with that, she walked away. An opening had occurred. She threw the rest to the wind, to take it where it pleased.

What a day! Openings everywhere. Either every part of this was just meant to be, or she had an amazingly active guardian angel out there somewhere.

15

AFTER ONLY A FEW months of living in Rural, Ruby felt like she had rejoined the human race.

A smaller human race, to be sure, but there was life there. It was indeed filled with life, wonderful characters and great learning.

In no time at all, she had five new clients! Stace practically brought them with her. As soon as she learned that she could look at things differently and started to comport herself in a different and more confident way, her friends asked what her secret was. They couldn't get enough of Ruby and spread the word to their friends.

Buying a bike with her first counseling check, Ruby biked to work at Reardon's every day. True to her word, Reardon did not care when she showed up. She paid her for four hours and was grateful for the help.

She loved arriving at Reardon's shop before everyone was up. It was the best time to learn how to bake new desserts. It turned out that Reardon was the baker of choice for many individual special occasions, as well as supplying the area restaurants with delectable pies, cakes and cookies. Because of all the special events, many times there was something new to try out.

If Reardon was thinking out a new cake as she went, Ruby would just observe her in silence. Fairly quickly, she got the hang of the donuts, though, and could get right to work on those, freeing up Reardon to make the fancier stuff. She felt giggly and entertaining around Reardon. She could make her laugh at the drop of a hat and quickly realized how much Reardon needed and loved that laughter. In a funny way, she felt as needed and received there—at Reardon's making donuts—as she had ever felt anywhere.

Ruby gave to her therapy clients, opening up their minds and hearts. She loved to watch them grow. With Reardon, she gave and received back in equal measure. With Reardon in her life, she had balance.

From time to time, when Ruby reflected on her circumstances, there was only one thing missing in her life and it wasn't love. It was sex. She'd always found pleasure in her prowess in that department, but there were moments when she would look down at her body, under an apron with flour on it, and wonder if everything south of the border was still even working after being dormant for so long.

Careful what you wish for, she heard something inside her say.

16

THE DAY CAME WHEN Ruby knew she had reached the end of what she could do to the house on her own. She had taken a lot of the previous personal effects out of her room and put them in the barn. She had arranged her own stuff and spruced up her bedroom.

Frank slept in the front room on the second floor. After Clara died, he had abandoned the master bedroom down the hall for good. Ruby had added some life to the room he was now in. She had changed the curtains, taken out the file cabinets and repainted the room. But she always did these things slowly and not so he'd feel misplaced.

The nice thing about that room was the separate staircase that went up to it. This made the room more private for Frank.

And when he was ready to move to the back house, she thought it would be a nice room to see her clients in. The separate entrance from the house would benefit everyone. For now, clients came to the barn, which worked but could definitely be improved on!

With some money trickling in, it seemed the time had come to hire Flipper for some additional help. Frank had just mentioned to her that he had just seen the boy. He was needing money for the swim team, so he was doing his "asking around" junket. Frank took his number and asked Ruby if she wanted him to call.

"What is his actual name anyway?" she asked.

"What does that mean?" Frank eyed her curiously.

"Nothing. I just wondered," she said, not willing to share the name Flipper, her code name for the kid. What if he really turned out to be a short kid who looked a little bit porpoise-like? Then it would really be mean. Maybe his body wouldn't look like that. After all, he swam competitively. But in Rural, Wisconsin, who was the competition? That could mean just about anything.

"His name is Daniel Proctor."

"Hmm. Sounds like a dentist."

"Is that a bad thing? Should I call him? We do need some drilling done." Frank's humor was sly but sweet.

"Yeah. See if he can come by tomorrow in the late

afternoon."

The next afternoon, Ruby was up sitting on the roof in her favorite spot reading when a man walked up and came through the front gate. He hadn't spotted her on the roof yet, but she could look at nothing else.

Flipper wasn't even remotely porpoise-like. He was tall with beautiful big shoulders, dark wavy unkempt hair and piercing blue eyes.

Holy shit, that guy is gorgeous, she thought. And she knew that he didn't know it yet. Maybe girls his age liked him. She was fairly sure of that. But they would have no idea of his capabilities. She could tell what they were from the roof! Oh my. She fought to keep her libido from doing the watusi.

Then, breathing as normally as she could under the circumstances, she scrambled back in through the window and rushed down to meet him.

17

"HI THERE. DANIEL? I'M Ruby...Woah!"

With no previous knowledge that her front step could even be tripped over, she stepped right out over it missing the step all together, clumsily falling into the young man's arms. They both laughed as he sort of righted her back up on her feet.

"Yes ma'am. I'm Daniel. Pleased to meet you." Ruby ordinarily would have taken umbrage at being called ma'am. But he said it so sexy that she wanted to ask him to say it to her again, about a hundred more times.

Daniel might or might not have known it, but when she had fallen and they had touched, Ruby instantly knew she was playing with dynamite here. Their chemistry was off the charts. He might have felt it too, she reasoned, but he was a bit innocent, so he might not have known what to do with it.

Ruby knew all sorts of stuff to do with it. She had to stop herself from thinking of new things to do with it, every second they were standing there. She had to change the subject right away.

"Gee Daniel, I'm not sure you can work with someone as graceful as I am! What do you think?"

He smiled. Oh. My. God. He looked right at her and it went directly to her groin. She thought she was going to faint. This was not going well.

Still smiling, he said, "I think I'm up for the challenge. But can I be the one with the hammer?"

He teased her this soon! She loved it. "Uh. Yeah." She was at a loss for words. She was at a loss for blood flow above her waist. She laughed out loud. She was, at this very moment, worse than any of those rabid dogs of men in bars who had ever wanted her. This poor boy was being mentally violated in every way imaginable and he hadn't even stepped inside the house yet!

She took him out back so that they could talk to Frank. But Frank was watching Daniel, not her. It was then that she realized he was sizing up the boy's intentions, while not seeing hers. Whatever he saw there seemed to placate him, for he instantly showed Daniel a list of what needed to be done with his back house. He explained to Daniel that he was getting anxious to start working on that building. He told them both that he was anxious to move out there.

Ruby was touched by Frank giving her another topic to concentrate on. "Of course. We actually need a lot of things done all over the house but if you want to move out there, it's as good a place to start as any."

She went inside the house while they talked and made everybody lemonade. She got her breathing under control, for the eightieth time. This is crazy, she told herself. He has got to be at least ten years younger than you! He is still in high school! Get a grip on yourself, Tuesday!

By the time the two men re-entered the house, Ruby had regained her peace of mind. Or a piece of her mind anyway. Or had stopped thinking of Daniel as a piece. One of those had happened.

She thought of the girls she was therapeutically working with. Her clients were his age. They were so unclear about so many things. Yet she respected them and their process. Flipper deserved her respect as well.

In the discussion outside, any tension between the two men had dissolved. Frank came in with his hand around Daniel's shoulder, happy to be hiring him.

"Just listen to his terms, Ruby!" he said excitedly. "I have a feeling we can meet them!"

"Really? What are they?"

"I'm willing to work for you whenever you need me and I can do it. You can pay me whatever you like and if you need to take time to pay me, that's no problem at all. No one's had any work for me for a while and this looks like fun."

"Wow," she said, "you drive a hard bargain, Daniel. You're hired."

"Thanks," he said, feeling the need to smile at her again. Ouch. If he kept feeling that need, things could get out of hand.

"Let the games begin!" she said, with a flourish.

18

RUBY WAS FEELING AT home in a lot of places. She felt at home in her home with Frank. Their friendship had steadily grown, with the shared project of the property between them. Ruby didn't ever want to stop working on it. She loved the transformational quality of it. Whenever one thing got done and came into line, some part of her mind fell into place as well and opened up to new life at the same time. She couldn't imagine it ever stopping! She just wanted to keep going forever.

Frank felt the same way. Time and time again he would sit down, explaining to her what could be done with a wall or a floor. Once she got his image, she always thought it was a great idea. And her enthusiasm wasn't false. Frank had great taste and instincts. Knowing that he got high as a kite whenever he thought up the next phase down the road, she would scream, "Let's do it!"

Speaking of high, she was getting high again! So the world had regained its occasional rosy hues. That was nothing but good. To Ruby, consciousness was a great place to be. But being in an altered state was pretty great too. Now she had more than one choice.

Months ago, she had gone into Milwaukee to meet this woman, Shelby. A friend from college, Kate, had hooked them up. Ruby had gone to meet Shelby, feeling a little trepidation, since in truth she had never really liked Kate all that much. In fact, she liked her so little that she ordinarily would have bagged the meeting, since it had been arranged by Kate. But the larger truth was that she wanted to get out and around in Milwaukee and be a wild woman from time to time, so it was worth at least a first meeting.

When she first met Shelby at a bar in Milwaukee, she immediately liked her. Shelby was a dark, seriously exotic beauty with a wild, ribald sense of humor. She threw men off their balance with all of her opposing qualities. Once they were floored, Shelby then decided what she wanted to do with them or whether or not she could do without them. Ultimately, she could do without any of them.

That was the quality Ruby prized the most in a girl friend,

especially a partying one. She wanted Milwaukee to be about a good time, no preaching, no dire ramifications, no girlfriend that she had to continually lift out of the doldrums. She wanted to hit the night with fun and style. Shelby was the perfect tour guide.

Having a comfortable trust fund and having lived in Milwaukee most of her life, Shelby knew most all of the regulars and where all their skeletons were buried.

Two immediate things told Ruby that Shelby was a keeper. The first was her directness and her ability to be around another woman. When they first met, Shelby immediately gasped as she said, "NOW look what the cat dragged in. You are one gorgeous hunk of woman!"

Ruby laughed. "I'm staring down that same tunnel the other way, girlfriend. You are a knock out!" They laughed and hugged.

Ruby knew her looks were a factor as she interacted with men. She also knew to watch closely for women who were at all intimidated by her. There were a few times when she had missed the signs and ended up spending time with a woman who was in reality rooting against her, in large or small ways.

She determined long ago that life was too short for those women. She might end up alone in life or with a harem of twelve men. But whatever her choices turned out to be, she wanted women around her that could hang with any choice she made.

Shelby could hang. She had stated the obvious about Ruby's beauty so that Ruby was free to state the same about hers. Then they could get on with it, thick as thieves.

There were some limits to the relationship. Ruby wouldn't confide something to Shelby, for instance, that was half as deep or personal to her as what she would talk to Reardon about. On the other hand, that kind of friendship wasn't going to be what Shelby and Ruby had, so they accepted what was and had a lot of fun together whenever Ruby wanted to get away.

The other thing that worked between them was their frankness. Once they had gotten together on several occasions, Ruby felt comfortable enough to tell Shelby that she really didn't like Kate, the mutual friend that had introduced them via long distance.

"That cow! I never liked her!" Shelby screamed. "What a nut job! In fact, I can't believe I ever agreed to meet you with her as the set up."

"Me either! I would have turned the car around with all my second thoughts but I was on a bus at the time!" They both laughed.

Ruby had since gotten a used car that one of her clients had found out about for her, so the bus was no longer necessary. But she still sometimes took it for a day in Milwaukee and then stayed with Shelby.

"Still," Shelby reflected. "She did do us a solid. Hey, let's call and thank her and be done with it."

Shelby was impulsive like that. So they called and thanked Kate, making faces at each other from different rooms on different extensions. They hung up, did a couple of lines of coke that Shelby had saved for them and headed off to a cool bar.

The very first time Ruby met Shelby, she told her she was really missing some weed. Shelby's reaction was immediate. "Mi loco weed es su loco weed!" she exclaimed.

"You are so deeply international," Ruby deadpanned.

"Ain't I though?" Shelby quipped. But she had sent her home on the bus with some nice weed. Some of the best Ruby had ever had.

Yep. Doesn't pay to underestimate Wisconsin, she thought.

19

EVERY TIME RUBY CAME back from Milwaukee, she was stocked. She wanted to meet Shelby's best friend, Riley, who was her supplier.

"He is very private. I'm getting him ready for you," Shelby would always say. "But when the time is right…"

For her next Milwaukee visit, Ruby drove up early on a Saturday morning. Reardon was closing the shop for a few days, so that she could take her two kids on a camping trip.

For Ruby to stay home while the shop was closed made even less sense. Frank and Daniel were going to be working on Frank's floor in the back. They had to take out that tree, which was in bad shape anyway and remove the roots that had grown under the floorboards. This would most likely mean they would both have their shirts off.

Ruby could easily stick around with Frank's shirt off, but with Daniel's shirt off? That boy was dancing around eighteen years old! She wasn't sure what age exactly, but what difference did it really make? Barely legal! She had better get the hell out of Dodge. Daniel with his shirt off was better than anything she could get in Milwaukee, but she often stopped and counted silently, just to get her breath back from imagining...

Yep, she thought. She still had some scruples left. However. Just to play it safe, Ruby left town before Daniel came over. before she could find out if she was right or not about those remaining scruples.

Life was holding a surprise for Ruby, though. She could feel energy changing and starting to swirl. Once in Milwaukee, Shelby showed her into her apartment. She looked decidedly excited about something.

"Wassup?" Ruby inquired, immediately.

"Oh nothing. Just thought you might want to have some lunch, that's all!"

Ruby knew that just having lunch with her wouldn't make her friend this giddy.

"And?"

"Would it be okay if we went to Riley's house?"

Ruby let out a little happy scream! "About time! Let's go!"

20

NEITHER RILEY NOR HIS house disappointed.

When Shelby brought Ruby to the door and rang the bell, she was visibly excited. Ruby knew that Shelby was not only excited about introducing them. She was also obviously excited to see her friend. Though she hadn't known Shelby long, she knew her enough to know that she leaned on no one. Her independence was strongly in her nature. She prized it above almost anything. But Riley was clearly her sea change.

The outside of the house didn't attract the eye per se. It was part of a condo complex that was obviously upscale but a bit generic from the looks of it. And then...

Riley came to the door and opened it. "Well, at last it happens. Ruby. You must be the gem I've been hearing about."

Riley was a large black man, tall in stature in both body size and general imposing qualities. Though not what you would call a handsome man, he was magnetic. Time would show him to be the smartest and best thinker Ruby had ever met, but even now, the wisdom, the humor and the lovely, shocking intensity were all so obvious in this man that they nearly knocked her over. She also instinctively knew that the truth was all Riley would allow in this house. Posers who mistakenly got in here would either be escorted out or easily pummeled down to size.

In a rush, she realized that the part of LA that she missed and hadn't allowed herself to realize that she missed was here, completely present and fulfilled in this man. The urbanity, the worldliness, the sardonic pleasures.

Ruby had no idea why she was doing this with a total stranger but she rushed forward and hugged him. He didn't meet her enthusiasm but he hugged her back and when she pulled away, he was smiling, in spite of himself.

"You brought a real live wire to my abode, Shell. Well then, you two might as well troop in."

Giving Shelby a hug, he led the way. Ruby was in complete shock at Shelby letting him call her Shell. Wow. Her rules were clearly different where this man was involved.

Once she could tear herself away from staring at Riley, she noticed she was in a pied-a-terre par excellence. With an almost

180 degree view of Milwaukee Bay, what had looked land bound from the outside looked airborne from the inside. You could see the boats coming and going, the tourists walking along the waterfront, the mansions on Lake Drive and the city for miles around. This was obviously a perfect vantage point for a man who wanted to be king of all he surveyed without having to step down into it.

"I could stare at this view for weeks," Ruby said in astonishment.

"You've just summed up my life pretty well," Riley snorted.

"Riley G, take us on a tour!" Shelby urged him. "Looks like you've moved some stuff around."

"You're half right. Stuff has been moved around, but I wasn't the one to do it, as you might have guessed. I hired a few young lads to do my heavy lifting."

"And was that view a good one, too?" Ruby joked, instantly feeling that she had gone too far. Riley looked at her and managed to convey both that she had overstepped initial boundaries and that he would let it slide.

"Sadly, not so much," he said, with an insouciant disappointment playing over his face. "I must alter my selection process somewhat before I do it again."

They walked around the house, coming back to the living room where a table by the window was set and food was served.

"Look at that. Benson discreetly made lunch and then left for an hour or two. He must have been thinking I was entertaining on a more visceral level," he said to them. "Straight as a tiny old arrow, but he knows his way around a chicken salad."

"He knows his way around more than that!" Shelby said. "Benson has been taking care of Riley since God was a Jew!"

"Since God was a Jew? My. There goes our Shell, merrily and violently mixing her metaphors again!" Shelby punched him playfully in the arm.

Ruby felt swept into the light-hearted moment. "Okay, I have to ask. Riley G and Shell? Are these what, I don't know, pet names?"

"Oh God no," Riley added. "I've never had a pet and if I did, it wouldn't be her. She doesn't mind or obey." As he said this, he looked at Shelby with real love for the first time and Ruby saw his tender, quiet side, for an instant. She told herself that she would like to know him well enough to see it more often.

"G is his middle initial. I just stick it in there to remind him that he isn't his father…"

"As if I needed reminding!"

"Sometimes you do, my darling," Shelby said, showing that she could supersede him at times. "Oh, that, and the fact that it irks him somewhat."

"Yes, you know how it is. She needs to feel she can do that

from time to time. But that name sounds like I scratch records or whatever you call it." They all laughed.

Since he had given a little room to her, Shelby returned the favor by fessing up. "My parents given name for me was Shelley. I changed it to be more exotic and because I knew another Shelley in school that I loathed. As soon as I could get out of that school system, I left the name behind too."

"Hey, look who you're talking to," Ruby said in consolation. "I'm Ruby Tuesday, for pity sake." She expected them to laugh, but they nodded somberly.

"A pity, that," Riley intoned. "One imagines that you weren't in your right mind at the time. But we won't hold that against you. We're bigger people than that."

There was a pause and then they all started to laugh, forging a bond that Ruby somehow knew would never be broken.

Over lunch, Ruby asked and got the whole Riley story. He was one of the city's leading defense attorneys and had been for a long while. He had a few associates in his firm, "just to do the camera work," he quipped, but also clearly meant. His work was in the courtroom, not in the public eye. "Never in the public eye," he stated more than once for emphasis at different points.

"What if there is a camera in the courtroom?" Ruby wondered.

"I grin and bear it," he said.

"Not hardly!" Shelby interjected. "He looks down, at the judge and at the jury only, so most cameras give up on him."

Riley shrugged. "That does happen to be where the action is. I don't have to convince the court of public opinion. I only have to convince the jury."

"I for one would love to see you in action," Ruby said.

"Oh yes, let's go!" Shelby said, excitedly.

"Whee!" Riley said, dripping with sarcasm. "As lovely as you two creatures are, do you really have nothing better to do than to watch me mess with the heads of poor little jury members?"

"NO!" they both screamed in unison and laughed.

Later, over a second bottle of wine drunk only by the women—Riley didn't drink or smoke—he told them about the marijuana component of his life and how it had come in.

He was defending a grower, whom he liked and respected. The charges were bogus but at the time, it was a sticky situation and no one wanted to take the grower on or even be associated with him. But Riley agreed to meet with him and felt he was a good man and took the case. The judge knew that Riley had won the case after his arguments were completed, so he just slapped the grower's wrists and let him walk out, a free man.

From that point on, a different man came to his door every couple of months and left him a package. Riley told the grower that he didn't imbibe, but the grower just smiled and said, "I know you don't. I also know you will know who to give it to."

Riley devised a system where he determined who to give it to, with research and background work - the most enjoyable part for him. "Riley gave away pounds of this stuff to AIDS and cancer patients before medical marijuana was even a thing," Shelby pointed out proudly.

"Yeah and I still give it away to them because mine is better," he said softly.

"You give it all away?" Ruby asked. "What are you, Robin Hood?"

"That's Mr. Robin Hood to you, but no." He added. "I sell some. I wickedly charge to the skies if people can afford it."

As he spoke, Ruby could see why he was as good as he was at law and at anything he put his mind to. He had the finest, clearest lines in his head of acceptable and non-acceptable behavior. Those lines might not be the same as anyone else's, but that hardly mattered. Each line he drew was thinner than thin yet completely clear to him.

"Aren't you afraid that you would be turned in?" she asked quietly.

"Ah, but no one knows they are getting it from me," he said. "No one. It's built into the distribution. This is where Robin Hood meets Jason Bourne."

He and Shelby immediately launched into a dramatic bit,

lowering their voices and reciting simultaneously.

"People. Do you have any idea who you're dealing with? This is Jason Bourne. You are nine hours behind the toughest target you have ever tracked! Now I want everyone to sit down, strap in and turn on all you've got! That would mean NOW!"

Watching the Bourne movies was a must for them, they told her, and they did it all the time.

Riley explained that he had minions who did the deliveries but didn't go into more details except to add one thing.

"You, my new friend Ruby, must be the sole of discretion. You now know me. Few others do. But I have already determined that, what with your donut making and your having to listen to lovelorn teenage girls all day, you will be one of my freebies. There. Aren't you thrilled?"

Ruby felt shock at the details about her life having been found out and simply stated like that. As she looked to Shelby for answers, her friend looked a little pale. She turned to Ruby and said quietly, "Honest, Ruby. I didn't tell him any of that."

"You didn't have to." Riley said, enigmatically. He poured them some more wine and, smiling, sat back. The subject was closed.

21

———

BACK FROM MILWAUKEE FOR several weeks, Ruby still felt electrified. To be in Riley's presence had given her an energy transfusion that she wouldn't have believed. She could see that Shelby refueled her joie de vivre just by being around him as well.

Riley was as deliberate about whom he allowed into his life and his home as he was with everything else. He didn't take you in if he couldn't afford the energy transfer required. She desperately hoped that this amazing man would let her in. She realized that, already, she didn't really want to live without him in her life, though she hoped she wouldn't have to. For now, she was buzzing.

Almost flying, she raced into the donut shop the next morning at the very first minute of prep time-four o'clock on the dot. Reardon pulled up and came in, shocked to see her there, waiting.

"Well, this is a surprise, darlin'! Even when you can't sleep, you don't make it here this early!"

They hauled in flour and sugar sacks together and started to bake with gusto. It was early spring which, in Wisconsin, still did a pretty good imitation of being winter. The air was cold but hauling twenty-five-pound flour and sugar sacks quickly took good care of that. A lot of special orders were flowing in. In particular this morning, a birthday cake, ten dozen cookies and some baked cinnamon loaves on top of their regular large list of restaurant orders.

It was hard work and Ruby loved it. She loved when she could work alongside Reardon and relieve her of having to make or even oversee whole recipes that she was now capable of making, and in any quantity! Reardon watched out of the corner of her eye and though she almost never corrected her, Ruby knew she wouldn't let her do something horribly wrong or something that couldn't be corrected, especially with a big order. Money wasn't so overflowing that a big mistake could be afforded.

But Ruby, energized by her Milwaukee meeting, took some chances that morning and started to probe a little into Reardon's life.

She asked Reardon when her husband Drew had passed away. It was four years ago and quite suddenly. Because he was a workaholic, he was seldom home. Reardon really raised their kids, Drew Jr. and Trudy, herself. Even though her kids missed their dad, it was only peripherally.

Reardon and Drew hadn't been soul mates. She didn't actually say that, but it came through everything she said about him and their marriage. They had married too young to ascertain their true level of connection. And by the time they realized they missed that level of intimacy, neither of them knew how to go back and get it. It was too late for that.

Reardon told her that the only thing she missed, still to this day, was sleeping in their bed next to him. She still hated to sleep alone. Sometimes after he left, the kids would crawl in with her and she was content beyond words. But now, they were way past the age for that.

"I could loan you Mutt! He gives off a whole lot of body heat!" Ruby suggested.

"Ah, but it would only be a loan. Besides, I'm more into the human kind of companionship. No offense to you, Mutt." They looked over at Mutt, who came to work with Ruby some days— when he could tear himself away from Frank and Daniel. Mutt was her dog, through and through, but it took a village and Mutt liked everyone in his village a whole lot.

"Hey, how was that camping trip a while back with the kids? How did that go?" Ruby and Reardon often didn't track their conversations in a linear fashion. With such immediate work in front of them every day, they would sometimes follow up on a story way after the fact.

Reardon was kneading a huge mound of dough but paused briefly as she thought back about it. "I guess it went fine," she said with some resignation. Punching the dough with a bit of hostility, she added, "as long as you weren't counting on eye contact of any kind."

The kids had brought their phones with them, which Reardon couldn't talk them out of, plus there were campers nearby with kids their ages, so they had to check them out. They came back for dinner, though sometimes bringing their friends back with them. Ruby laughed about that, assuring Reardon that her dinner probably smelled and tasted better than any other dinner on the grounds.

After that, Reardon was lost in thought for a bit as they worked. Then she finally spoke again.

"But they love me. I know that." She smiled and exhaled out her frustrations.

"I see it! All the time!" Ruby gushed. "Oh buddy, I see their eyes and there is pure adoration in there. I work with kids a lot these days, as you know. And you can pretty much throw the top, day to day layer out. It's the layer underneath that is running the show. Drew and Trudy are busy acting their ages, but you have them for the long haul. They will always be near you. They adore you." The words had come out in a rush, but Ruby meant them and she knew she was right.

Reardon smiled at the outburst, as she sprinkled out some more flour on the counter and pressed the dough into it to absorb it. "I'm glad for that. I know I love them."

Ruby knew that for Reardon, simply bestowing the word love said a whole world. Reardon didn't love a lot of people but when she loved, it ran deep.

"But times change. Both kids can drive themselves everywhere. I've lost them right there, at least for a while," she chuckled.

"How does that come into play? You only have one car and you use it first and foremost."

"Ah, but you are forgetting one thing. The fact that they can drive also means that all of their friends can drive, too!"

They both laughed. "You got a point there," Ruby said, taking out four racks of cookies from the convection oven and putting in four more. "Remember when you first got your license? I had my brother's old beat-up car. But man oh man. I drove all over, just to drive. Man, that was liberation city to me! Luxurious privacy," she stopped her work momentarily, still savoring the feeling.

Reardon smiled. "Yep. I remember. So they are lost to me right now."

Ruby tested the oil temperature to start the donuts. "They'll be back. They'll always be back."

22

———

BUOYED BY THAT TALK and knowing that Reardon was a woman of few words but also a woman that could use a little more company from time to time, Ruby picked a weekend night that she wasn't heading into Milwaukee and one that Trudy and Drew were going to be out to suggest to Reardon that she could come over and cook for her for a change. She had been to their house before, but only to bring in takeout. This would be different. Reardon's face showed a bit of dubiousness, but she immediately said yes.

Over beef fillets with goat cheese and balsamic syrup and pasta mixed with gourmet bread crumbs and prosciutto, Ruby managed the impossible and got Reardon a little tipsy. This wasn't a spontaneous act on Ruby's part. She knew she needed that extra element to have the talk she had wanted to have with her friend from the day they met.

While Reardon was finishing second helpings of the great food-two of Ruby's specialties—Ruby sized her up.

Reardon wasn't a handsome woman, by the world's standards, but she had accepted that about herself a long time ago. She was kind and caring and she had love pouring out of her.

Those that she loved knew it and felt it, as a constant river flowing between them. And those that she didn't love yet could still feel that loving potential inside her and hoped for some of it to come their way. Ruby saw this when the two of them delivered things to people who had known Reardon for a long time. She was quiet and kind to everyone and more than a few people yearned for more time and attention from her. She obviously still had a lot of love to give. But to whom?

Ruby poured her a little more wine. Reardon had given up resisting the pours. Ruby braced herself and started in slowly.

"So, Drew has been gone for almost five years now."

"Yeah, just about."

"Aren't you lonely at all? Wouldn't you like to be with someone again?"

Reardon shook her head, partly to clear it. "Oh you know. Sex is sex. And besides, my life is full and busy and there's the kids and who has time and who is around anyway that I could even imagine myself with?"

Her sudden tirade of reasons delivered at warp speed made them both sit back and laugh.

"Got your whole list of reasons there, huh?" Ruby gently kidded her.

"Apparently so!" Reardon said.

Ruby spoke softly now, mentally shrugging off the wine and in full therapy mode. "Might there be another reason that you didn't add to your list?"

Reardon didn't know what was coming but she looked scared. "Okay Sherlock. Inform me."

"My thought is that maybe there isn't a man out there for you. But maybe… there might be a woman?"

There was a silence. There was so much to add, but Ruby didn't say anything. This was a time to let the silence work. She kept quiet but looked down at her plate, letting Reardon have her privacy.

When she looked up minutes later, Reardon wasn't speaking, but a tear was rolling down her cheek. She looked scared, as if the world might open up and swallow her.

Ruby spoke, quietly again. "You never have to confront this, my wonderful friend. Your secret is as safe with me as it has been with you for all of these years. I've known it from the moment I met you."

Reardon was suddenly alarmed and suspicious. "But how could you..."

Ruby took the moment back down to quiet. "That doesn't matter. I see things in people. We can talk about that another time if you want to.

"But right now," she continued, reaching across the table and taking Reardon's hand. The touch was electrifying—not from chemistry but because it was the most intimate the two women had been. Ruby wanted that feeling to be present; to support what she was telling her boss and friend.

"I want you to know some things. First of all, your secret, if you want it to stay that way, could not be in safer hands. It is yours to share or not. Plus, I want nothing to impinge on what we have together. I want to be alongside you till your last breath."

She wanted to lighten things up a bit, so she added, "whether you are a tired, lonely old hag or you have found someone to love, I'll still be there."

A rainbow of a smile escaped through Reardon's tears.

Ruby continued. "I'm not gay. Though I'll tell you this. I'd be having a lot of fun if I was! I love women. I have loved and still love so many friends who are gay. And I love anyone who has the courage to love whoever they love."

She kept holding her hand. Reardon was crying but saying

nothing, so she continued, knowing that Reardon was flooded with thoughts and feelings but could still hear her.

"Ree," using a nickname that she had recently given to Reardon and then, only when the two of them were alone so it didn't spread. "You are a rock for all of us. Lonely and tired, but a rock."

"Nice," Reardon uttered.

Ruby laughed. "Yeah, it is a delightful self-image, I'll grant you that. A lonely, tired rock. Hmm. Pretty! But hey, you did what you were supposed to do. You performed the heterosexual ritual and you were prepared to give your life to it. But you don't have to anymore. Don't you see? You already gave at the office!

"And wouldn't you like to just see if this is what you have been wanting? To see if there is an Angelina Jolie out there for you?" she coaxed.

"I would never go for her," Reardon said. Both women were aware that, with that comment, she was finally owning up to the truth of what was being discussed.

Ruby started to chuckle. "See? This is progress! You've set the bar low! Less for all of those potential dates to live up to. Although I personally think you are shortsighted with no taste. I'm straight and I'd do Angelina Jolie in a sandstorm!"

She had gotten Reardon to laugh with that. She knew they were going to be okay from then on. Then, Reardon suddenly looked very serious.

"But there's no way. My kids..."

"Your kids will take their cue from you. If you are embarrassed, they will be too. If you are confident and easy going about it, they will learn that too. Mostly, they will see you as a woman who deserves to be happy as much as anyone else.

"And besides, who is telling them anything yet? Great honk, we haven't even gotten you a date yet! I haven't checked lately, but I think you have to at least kiss the girls first before you introduce them to the family!"

They laughed and then Reardon sat very still. Ruby waited her out. Finally, she spoke, a little shakily.

"So suppose I decided to throw caution to the wind. And I'm not even saying yet that I would! But if I did, where am I supposed to find this woman in Waupaca, Wisconsin? Got an answer for that, Sherlock?"

"Well, as a matter of fact, you aren't supposed to find her in Waupaca. Who wants to start that close to home? I have a few ideas. Take your time and I'll come up with something."

Ruby stood up to take the plates to the kitchen. Reardon's hand stopped her, shaking her head no. She stood up and faced her.

"First time you saw me, huh? I must be some kind of open book."

"You're not an open book at all. But I hope you will be,

when the right one comes along."

And with that, they hugged. Not for the first time but with an openness that meant the world to both of them. When they pulled back, they confirmed that they were both sobbing, so they went back to hugging.

Later on, doing dishes together, Reardon asked.

"So. Were you serious about Angelina?" "Serious as a heart attack. When you get big in the international gay circles, maybe you could arrange that for me."

"Are there international…?"

"Of course not! Don't be an idiot. But yeah, I'd do her. And we'd have big fun! Although, okay. I did stretch the truth. About the sandstorm part. Ick. But Angelina and a five-star hotel? Deal me in!"

Reardon shook her head. "As you would say, what an interesting visual!"

They laughed.

23

WHATEVER THE DAY BROUGHT, Ruby could fall back at night into the lovely ritual of making and having dinner with Frank. Sometimes Daniel stayed but never automatically. He was a polite kid and he never assumed. In fact, she could sense a potential good energy reader in him. She could train him and he'd be reading people very well in no time. She could train him in a lot of things...

But her safety net, when impure thoughts threatened to overtake her, was to focus on the beautiful bond that had begun to solidify between the two men. It wasn't a stretch to say that Daniel was the son Frank never had. It wasn't a stretch because it was obvious.

Ruby had been there when Daniel brought over his tools

for the first time to show Frank and to start to use them. Frank had filled her in earlier on the story of Daniel being close to his grandfather, who was a woodworker and did carpentry as well to pay the bills. Their bond was strong and when he died, he left Daniel the most important and enduring legacy he had. He left him all of his tools.

As they looked at the tools, Frank had taken each one out, holding it and asking about it. And he was right to handle it that way as Daniel remembered stories about each tool, stories that made both men stop and take moments of silence to contemplate.

As the two men shared each story, with Daniel starting them and Frank asking a question or two to bring out more of what he knew Daniel wanted to talk about, the bonding grew between them. Ruby looked to the heavens often and gave thanks for the divine symmetry that this building provided. Everyone was getting what they wanted out of this, beyond anything they could have sought out.

Sometimes, in the best of times, life was really like that.

The months had passed with dinner being a quiet event each night, sometimes between the three of them and sometimes just the two of them.

Frank picked up a new hobby in his old age and that was grilling! Clara had never liked a grill—too messy to clean. She told Frank it was only one step removed from burning leaves in their yard, a Wisconsin custom that she loathed and wanted no association with.

Out of respect for her wishes, Frank had slowly and completely forgotten over the years that he liked to grill until one day when he and Ruby were at the hardware store getting supplies. There were grills up front.

"Ooh, do you like to grill, Frank?" she asked. "I have never really learned but it seems like fun. What say you?"

The thought moved through Frank until it hit a place from long ago where he rediscovered that he had always wanted to grill. The biggest smile ever started to spread across his face, making him look about thirty years old.

"Yeah, I'd love to grill. I mean, I'd really LOVE to grill."

Expressions like that came few and far between from Frank. Ruby loved that her idea had been the cause of one.

"Let's do it then!" she chirped happily. "And we can teach Daniel, too. Every man should know his way around a grill!"

Frank knew she was teasing a bit, but they soon found the perfect simple grill and loaded it up. Ruby was having a good month, having added a few adults to her counseling practice. Slightly older meant that they could afford a bit more for their sessions on her sliding scale. She couldn't think of a better reward for that financial uptick.

This was yet another domestic thing that she and Frank could do together. He stayed out of her way as much as possible, which worked out beautifully for Ruby. With as independent a nature as she had, she was always grateful to spend a little time with Frank. And she was grateful that he allowed her to reach for his company, rather than hanging around too much.

She knew that Frank was very content and even the thought of that made her happy. Not truly a dog man, he and Mutt had found a connection. He didn't goo goo ga ga over him, but they were friends. And then there was his surrogate son, Daniel. Whenever she totaled Daniel's hours to pay him, she knew that he was there long beyond the hours he clocked in and it was because of the extra hours the two men spent just talking and being together.

Tonight, they decided to celebrate for no reason, with steaks and corn on the grill. Though corn was not yet completely in season, it was still a treat. Ruby could write a whole book on Wisconsin corn. Any Wisconsin native could! If you had ever bitten into spankin' fresh Wisconsin corn, you would be willing to brave those winters just to live near it. Sweet like no other corn in the world, it had no equal. Except, of course, Wisconsin tomatoes. Sweet and unlike any other tomatoes she had ever tasted as well.

When she was young, her mother used to make tomato

sandwiches. Upon moving back to Wisconsin, Ruby had resurrected that practice. She had one almost every lunch when she was working. No way to imagine a sandwich with just tomatoes in it—anywhere except in Wisconsin.

But it turned out there was an actual reason to celebrate, or at least commemorate a passing of sorts.

Frank pulled out three steaks and said to her, "I've asked Daniel to come tonight."

"Oh? A special occasion?"

"You could call it that. The house in back is ready. It is airtight and I'm ready to move in. I moved the heater from the basement out there and it is very cozy and nice."

Ruby didn't know how she felt. She knew she wasn't pushing Frank out. He had wanted to move back there all along. She knew he was a proper man. Though they had successfully quelled talk in their little town of them living together in sin, she knew he had been in want of a little more autonomy.

It was she who felt the indecision about it. Ruby felt the house was a little big for one person and she loved coming in late or leaving early and knowing that Frank was in the house. But this was what he wanted, even though she couldn't help but ask one more time.

"Frank. Are you sure this is what you want?"

His sigh told it all. "Yes, Ruby, this is what I want. And

besides, you can't keep seeing clients in that drafty barn. You and all of them will get double pew-monia."

They both laughed at his funny expression. Ruby bought some champagne and they went home to celebrate.

It was a fine feast. Though Frank usually helped her with the dishes, he was anxious to go out back and get situated. Daniel offered to take his place.

"Fine. That'll be fine." In an excited but rare show of emotion, Frank hugged Daniel first, then Ruby. "Thank you, dear girl," he said, reaching up and patting her face gently. "You have changed my life into something splendid."

As he left, Ruby turned to the sink with tears in her eyes. She knew she could thank Frank for the exact same thing. But it would mean more when she could find the right moment to say it back.

24

SHE TURNED AWAY FROM the sink and looked at Daniel. The two of them had avoided being alone together for months and instantly all the heat was back. He looked a bit older and even more handsome, if that was possible.

"You do a lot of that, you know," he said. "Change lives. You sure have changed mine. In point of fact, you have rearranged everything inside me." He moved a step closer to her. "And I can't go back."

"Daniel, we've been through this."

"Have we? Let me say my peace for a minute. You have at least a minute to spare for me, don't you?" He patted the chair that Frank had just left and she sat down. The fact that they were even closer made it hard to concentrate.

"I'm in my last year of high school. And this is a year past when most of my classmates were there. I was missing a few credits so I needed one more semester. I decided to stay for the whole year so that I could swim competitively for one more season. I'm taking very few credits this last semester and then I will start taking a few courses at a woodworking school in Wausau. I plan to become a furniture builder. After this school year is up, I will move over to that school full time in the fall."

"That is so great, Daniel!"

"Shhh," he interrupted her, "no one said you could talk."

This was unbearably sexy, but it did have the effect of shutting her up.

"The most important thing I want you to know is that I am moving in with my brother as soon as I finish high school. I'm eighteen now and I will be nineteen the month I graduate. So I am an adult and will be a graduate, fair and square. And I believe, if I'm not mistaken, that the rule book says once I am an adult, there is nothing to stop me from doing any thing...or any one...I want.

"Oh, and one other thing. I already know some furniture makers that might take me on when I'm through with woodworking school, so what are you going to do? I'm still going to be around. Plus that barn of yours needs some serious help and I'm starting to meet some guys who could help me with that. But with your budget, that could take years."

They looked at each other for a long time; no one breathing.

"Eighteen, huh?" she said, with a small smile.

He returned the same smile. "Adult and everything."

"Not as adult as me."

"How do you know?" Their laughter broke the ice.

"Thanks for telling me all of that."

"Don't thank me. I don't want your thanks. I just needed you to know."

"Food for thought."

"Food for something." They laughed again, this time with very little mirth in it, just easing down the tension.

She got up from the chair and turned to the sink, saying over her shoulder, "I'll finish these myself," in a tone that let him know the night was over.

As she started to wash the dishes, he walked up behind her and just stood. She could feel him there, not touching her. She couldn't do anything. She stood motionless, ready to fend him off if necessary. There was only one thing that she knew for certain. If they started, they wouldn't be able to stop.

He moved forward until their bodies were touching. Ruby seriously felt like she would faint. Her hands involuntarily gripped the sink. She knew he saw her doing that. He gently put his hands on her waist and kissed the back of her head.

And then he was gone.

When the front door closed, she tried to keep doing the dishes, but instead ripped off her gloves. The dishes could wait. It was time to be alone in her bedroom.

25

RUBY WAS BACK IN MILWAUKEE, sharing the huge sofa with Riley and telling him all about Daniel and what happened at the sink that night.

Riley whistled. "Ooh, girl. Who are you to turn that away? It's been eons since any guy has been that sexy with me!"

They were becoming good friends and she knew that Riley was the only one she could talk to about this. She also knew his lifelong penchant for privacy meant that one night stands had always been his style.

"Well, maybe they don't get all that sexy because they know they are on borrowed time when they get here. They don't have time to get it up!"

"Oh, they get it up all right. That's what they're here for. As soon as it goes down, it's time to call them a cab. Male sex is a bit more cut and dry than what you're describing."

"So what, do you have an account with a cab company or something?"

His smile confirmed it. "You do! Wow! That is so efficient! I think."

"You could learn a little from my demographic, young lady."

"Such as?"

"Such as sex does not require negotiation."

"Yeah, but this is different, Riley. This is a young guy who is delicate and we live in the same little town and..."

"I know that, honey. I know it's different. But from what you've told me, I think you're thinking of him as more delicate than he is. He's been holding his water pretty well up until now."

"So what are you saying?"

"I'm saying that you are veiling this whole thing in concern for him. From where I sit, you are as or more delicate than him. You both have a lot to lose and a lot to gain."

"So I should be dropping the earth mother angle?"

"There's definitely a lot of earth in there. But mother? Not so much!"

On the way home, she looked through the windshield and tried to stop thinking about the whole thing. Then a thought came to her mind, but not from her, fully formed.

"*He's not going anywhere. You aren't going anywhere. Don't be afraid.*"

The thought calmed her. But there was a strangeness to it. It was a good thought. It just hadn't been her thought.

26

THE NEXT TWO WEEKS with Reardon at the bakery passed with no mention of their talk. At first that felt right. But after a while, Ruby began to worry a bit. Although she knew that Reardon trusted her to keep their conversation private, she hoped her friend wouldn't take the whole conversation and tuck it back safely into her shell.

Was it time to up the stakes? She thought it was, so she waited for and found the right morning to press the issue a little.

"Hey Ree, I don't know if you recall a little talk we had the other night?"

"Hmm...Which little talk?" Reardon asked, but with a shy little twinkle in her eye.

"Never mind, smart ass. But since you know full well what I'm talking about, I wanted you to know that I did a little research. I asked my friend Riley to do a little research on nearby lesbian bars."

"WOAH!" Reardon hollered. Clearly the wording alone had made her practically swoon.

"Too fast and loose with my phrasing? Sorry. But here's the thing. Although I do believe an amazing woman, were she to amble into your donut shop on the highway, might fall in love with you instantly...what are the chances? Do we want to wait for those odds? Should we? I don't know about you, but I'd like this to happen for you before you're eighty!"

"You have a point there."

"Now. Turns out we've heard talk of two bars in or near Madison."

"Madison?" Reardon interrupted, her frustration growing. "Why Madison?"

"When have you ever been in Madison?"

"Never."

"I rest my case. Baby steps. Your secret is safe in Madison. It's possible any secret is safe in Madison! But we don't have to test that out."

"Okay. I'm with you so far."

"Okay. Of the two bars, one is more out of town and severely reeks of a biker bar ambience, which means it would scare me and give you a heart attack."

Reardon quietly responded, "I'm with you so far."

"This other one seems pretty cool. Riley has never heard anything bad about it and he is always up for a good bar gone wrong story. So I'm taking you there on Friday night."

"You? You're going?"

"Of course I'm going. Use your head. Well, at least for this portion of the entertainment.

"First of all, I happen to like gay bars, although I prefer the male variety more. Way better music. In my limited experience in lesbian bars, the women are either too shy or too drunk—and often not a pretty drunk at that. But, after having painted this bleak picture, I haven't been to one in awhile, so I'm up for it. And besides, aren't you forgetting the greatest reason for going with me?"

"What's that?"

"Who the hell else are you going to be going there with?"

"You make a great point, grasshopper."

"Besides, Ree, you don't know this yet, but you're going to like going to a bar with me. Everybody does. I'm a good person to go to a bar with.

"And I won't make you stay if you want to leave. Well, that is, unless I deem it to be for your highest and best good to stay a while longer. Then we'll stay."

"You sound a bit more like a dictator to me!"

"Should the need arise, my friend. Should the need arise."

27

FRIDAY NIGHT CAME. RUBY was spending time getting ready before picking up Reardon. She hadn't spent time primping since her days in LA. But tonight, she felt a quiet but very definite energy change moving around her and through her body. She had always read energy but this time, it was as if she was being directed. This energy was directing her. There was something else in the mix.

For instance, she had planned to look reasonably good and stay reasonably out of the way, subtly helping her friend without overplaying her hand. She knew how hard this was going to be for Reardon and she didn't want to pull focus.

But that wasn't the internal, energetic feedback that she was getting. The energy current was telling her to get dolled up. It seemed counter to what she was thinking but she couldn't seem to tone down the message. There was going to be a need for her to look her best. The translation she was getting was becoming perfectly clear.

She was going to be used for something tonight.

"Used? For what?" Ruby asked out loud. But that was what she kept getting. Since she had never been in the business of ignoring the psychic hits she got, even though this one seemed different or to be coming from a different place, she still followed its direction.

She took off her jeans and put on a black tight turtleneck and black pants, comfortable shoes—God bless those lesbians— and put her long, blond hair in a loose ponytail. A little eye makeup, a little light perfume, earthy and sensual. Looking in the mirror, the effect was quite stunning. She laughed, thinking that she looked better than she had in a long while.

She passed by Frank and Daniel in the kitchen on her way to the car. The kitchen had a great alcove with a comfortable little table to sit, chill and talk. The two men were doing just that. But talk stopped and two sets of jaws dropped as she walked in.

"Wow," Daniel was speechless. His heart looked like it might have stopped.

"They don't make girls like you around these parts," Frank laughed.

"Yep, they actually do! I'm from around these parts!" Ruby chirped, proudly. "And I've got the blisters to prove that I live here."

"Where are you off to?" Daniel finally uttered, cautiously, like the answer might hurt him.

"Out," she chirped quickly, in a slightly higher voice, like the one she used to use with her parents before leaving. "I'll tell you later. Too long a story. See ya!"

28

RUBY HAD NEVER SEEN Reardon dressed up before. And when she picked her up, she still hadn't. Reardon approached the car in a slightly nicer shirt than usual, but otherwise no other difference. Ruby smiled to herself. The vast majority of the lesbian lifestyle was going to be such a lovely, easy fit for her friend!

After talking about anything but their destination, they arrived, walked into the bar and took a seat. Ruby did a quick, relaxed scan. Not so different from any other slightly countrified bar, with the exception of no men to be seen. She smiled, confirming that they were at the right place. So far, so good.

She heard someone singing and only then noticed a karaoke machine set up in the corner.

"Good," she thought. Or was it her thinking that? *"You'll need that later."*

Now she was confused. The direction for the night that had started earlier with how to dress was continuing. It was as if she had a mission to complete here, tonight, in this bar, but she just didn't know what it was yet.

As they drank their initial drinks in silence, Ruby began to listen to a quiet fight taking place between two women a few seats away, behind her as she was turned to face Reardon. The two women were obviously a couple. Since it was still early and still fairly quiet in the bar, it didn't take the slightest strain to listen in. It would have been harder to not hear it.

One woman was trying to be what people in LA referred to as a lipstick lesbian, although she was not quite succeeding. She had on a dress and lots of cheap makeup. She clearly thought the dress made her look hip but it clearly didn't. Her partner was fairly butch to look at—slightly overweight, wearing overly large jeans and a sweatshirt, so the whole effect was a puffy one. And if puffy sweatshirt woman had any self-esteem, it wasn't on display tonight.

Puffy was saying, as she started to cry a little, "You always say that to me. That I need to be more unique and more interesting. But I don't know how to do that. Don't you think I'd do that if I knew how? Don't you think I'd do anything to make you happy?"

Lipstick harrumphed. "But you see? That proves my point! You can't be more interesting because you just aren't more interesting. That's the point! You shouldn't want it for me! You should want it for you! Don't you want to be more?! To be something? Anything at all?"

Puffy said, barely above a whisper, "I don't know how to be any more than I am. For you or for me." Lipstick turned away from her and blocked her out as Puffy said in the quietest of whispers, "I'm clearly not worth anything."

The deeply serious energy with which she said those last words shot through Ruby and shook her to the core. She knew immediately, without any question in her mind, that this woman was going to kill herself. She knew that her girl friend, Lipstick, didn't know it. They had had this same discussion many times before. That was clear.

But this time was different. If something wasn't done, this woman's days or even hours were almost over. Ruby sat still and open and read Puffy's energy. She could tell that this woman already had a plan. She was going to let her girlfriend off the hook by dying, imagining that her death would eek the last bit of love she could feel for her. The thought that her death would cause her girlfriend even one minute of sadness was now all she could hope for.

Ruby saw the whole thing playing out in front of her,

energetically and visually. She was flooded with what she needed to do. She knew for certain why she had been brought here tonight. And for the first time ever, she knew that it had been planned before she even had a clue.

Reardon had been listening too. Ruby turned to her.

"Look Ree, I know we are here for you tonight. But there are some things I suddenly need to do. You won't maybe understand them and I can fill you in later. But don't be surprised by anything tonight, okay? I have to do whatever it takes."

Reardon nodded. "I know you do. I don't know why. But I trust you. I always have and I always will."

Ruby felt a flood of relief. That directional energy that had brought her here had also directed Reardon to understand, even if she wouldn't know what she was seeing.

So much was not known and yet something was very definite about all of it. Someone's life hung in the balance and Ruby could do something about that. She could do something and she would. The stage was set. Like it or not, she was on.

Lipstick had turned back to Puffy and was continuing. "Yeah, well since we agree on your inability to do anything about yourself, I may just have to branch out tonight. See what else is out there for me. Or who else is!" she said with a flourish.

If Puffy is close to ending it, Ruby thought, she won't cry, she'll just slump. Puffy slumped.

Lipstick's bravado was as false as a three dollar bill.

Ruby read that. With a chill, she realized Lipstick had been sucking her confidence from Puffy's hide for a long time now. She had none of her own. She was a parasite. Okay. All information was set.

Now shit needed to start.

In a slightly too loud voice, Ruby beckoned the bartender over. "Whew. Friday night! My friend and I are just passing through but I've never been here before and it's Friday night and I feel like partying! Do you think I could buy everyone at the bar a shot of whiskey?"

The bartender, sensing the possibility of some real money being waved around said, "I don't see why not."

"Everybody okay with Jack Daniels?" she asked the eight women seated around the bar. They all looked slightly suspicious but they all nodded.

"Line 'em up then," she said, backing her voice down a bit in response to the suspicion. "Let's get this party started."

29

————

AS THE BARTENDER POURED and passed the shots around, each person stared at them. Ruby looked at everyone, picked up hers and downed it without even squinting.

Everyone kept staring at her. She picked up Reardon's and downed it.

"Gotta be careful of my friend here. She's the designated driver. If I fall down, she's the one that's got to drag my sorry ass to my house."

She was carefully indicating to everyone that they were not a couple, leaving Reardon open to the room if she wanted to be. Reardon tapped her and said quietly, "I don't drink stuff like this. I won't be able to handle it."

"I'll handle it for you. Don't worry about it."

"But what if you...I mean, I've never seen you..."

"You're gonna see a bunch of things tonight that you've never seen before. May never see again. But I'm on it. Keep the faith." With a wink, she sauntered away.

The whiskey was in her veins now and the plan was taking form. Each step would dictate the next.

She walked over to Lipstick and Puffy, putting a hand on each of their shoulders. Lipstick stiffened up at the touch. Puffy barely noticed it.

"Aren't you girls going to have those shots?" She looked at Lipstick. "You look like a girl who can handle her liquor." Lipstick took a sip and made a face.

Ruby laughed inwardly. God, this little parasite was so feebly transparent. She could have manipulated her right off a cliff.

And still might! The night was young.

"I don't know. I just find that, in this day and age, women are so much more interesting if they can hold their liquor." As she said "interesting," she changed her grip on Puffy's shoulder to a loving small stroke on her back. Lipstick couldn't see the motion but Puffy felt it. She was sure of that.

Lipstick, feeling the beautiful woman's attention drift away from her to Puffy, laughed with contempt. "She won't try that. You are wasting your breath."

"Oh, you never know," Ruby said lightly, still stroking Puffy's back, ever so slightly. "It would sure be interesting if she did. Maybe even just this once." She turned her attention to Puffy, leaning in to her almost imperceptibly while still addressing Lipstick.

"Today could be a brand new day." She nodded slowly to Puffy, as if they were in cahoots. "Might turn out interesting. Today can have absolutely nothing to do with yesterday." And with that, she lifted her hand off of Lipstick and kept the other one on Puffy.

That did the trick. Puffy downed the shot. Lipstick's mouth gaped open. A couple of the women who knew her applauded.

"Now. Wasn't that good?" Ruby's attention was all with Puffy now. Puffy felt the victory of it and started to look over at Lipstick, who would have gone off on her for it.

"You think maybe you and I should have another?" She stepped in front of Lipstick and filled up Puffy's vision so that Puffy couldn't see anything but her. Yes, she nodded slowly, a bit hypnotized.

Ruby signaled the bartender by putting up two fingers and then pointing them to the bar for two more in front of Puffy, all without taking her eyes off of her. They watched each other and drank them down together.

Weakly but indignantly, Lipstick protested. "You didn't

offer me another one." Ruby turned to her, as if just now remembering that she was there. "Oh, I'm sorry but I can't. You lost your chance to be interesting by just sipping it. I mean, who sips a shot?"

A couple of the women who had applauded earlier now laughed.

"I guess she dogged you there, Lauren."

"Yeah, she got your number."

Just then, Puffy leaned in toward her and whispered. "I'm feeling a little dizzy now. Could I go to the bathroom?"

"Of course. I'll be right there." Ruby said, all comforting.

"Hah!" Lauren barked out, in contempt. "Typical. See?"

Ruby stifled the urge to imagine what Lauren's face would look like after she punched it. Instead she said, with enforced lightness, "Don't you worry about a thing. You came here to enjoy. I'll take care of her. I started this. I'll handle it."

30

_____

IN THE BATHROOM, PUFFY was sitting on a chair, looking quite a bit the worse for wear. Ruby calculated her weight, the fact that she didn't drink much and that there were two shots in quick succession. Might throw up but probably would be okay. At any rate, she had her alone, which had been the point, and she could comfort her freely when she wasn't feeling that well, which had been the other point.

Things, all in all, were proceeding according to plan.

She also knew that Reardon would leave them alone and Lauren could never look weak in front of her friends, so she would leave them alone too.

"Look, I'm sorry I got you into this position. It's all my fault. You might have to throw up and that's okay if you need to, believe me. But until then, have some water." She pulled out a bottle of water from her purse. She always brought one with her when she went to bars. But it was usually for her.

On second thought, she took the bottle after Puffy had had a swig and she raised it to her lips too, watching Puffy as she did. She couldn't explain it, but knew it spelled out an intimacy of some kind between them.

She then handed it back to Puffy.

Puffy managed a little smile. "You don't have to apologize. That look on Lauren's face when I took that shot was the most fun I've had in...ever!" She laughed a little.

"So good to see you smiling! Can I know your name?"

"Well, everyone at work and here calls me Chase, my last name. But my first name is Claire."

"What would you like me to call you?"

A look passed between them. Feeling drunk but very comfortable, she said, "I think...Claire."

Bingo, Ruby thought. We've passed through something.

"Well, good. I like them both, but I was kind of hoping for Claire. It's really such a pretty name. It's Irish, isn't it?"

"I don't know. I think so. Wait a second, yeah. I think my ancestors were Irish!" She got a little happy, just thinking about that fact.

Ruby watched her bearing. She was still a bit slumped, but

more from whiskey than from defeat. She took the bottle back and pretended to drink, noticing that every time she did that, Claire would take a big swig right afterward. This woman was child-like. She wasn't uninteresting; she was just not fully developed yet. Ruby wanted her to have that chance. She pressed on.

"You know, back where I live, I have this friend, Frank. He was married for years and years to a woman named Clara. But I think Claire was his nickname for her. He slips up every once in awhile and calls her that. Man, he loved her so much. It's almost hard to imagine a person who could just adore you like he did her. To have someone care about you with no judgment, no conditions, just happy to be in your company."

Claire was still a little wobbly but listening and hearing every word. Then she shook it off.

"Nice story. But people don't love each other like that."

"People do!" Ruby raised her voice, purposely startling Claire momentarily. Claire blinked and sat up, still listening.

"People love like that all over the world, Claire. They have been loving like that throughout time. People have moved mountains for love. They have slayed dragons for love. Or, like my friend Frank and his Claire, they have lived quietly together for years with that kind of love."

"I can't believe it."

"But it's true. That kind of love exists. All over the place." Ruby said, touching a damp paper towel to Claire's forehead, helping her to come back from her fog.

"Maybe you and I, people like us, haven't found that love yet and maybe we never will. But we won't stop looking for it. And we won't settle for anything less."

As she said that, she nodded very gently and watched Claire begin to nod as well.

"You know, someone once told me that the true test of love is how you feel right after you've been with somebody. If you feel really horrible about yourself after you've been with someone, don't ask another question. That person isn't right for you to be with." With that, she went momentarily from nodding to almost imperceptibly shaking her head. Claire did the same, without being aware of it.

"And if you feel good about yourself after being with a person, that means they helped you to feel that way. You want to keep going back to them and being around them. There's something in that relationship that is right."

Ruby knew she was getting through. She also knew that she didn't have much time left. They had been in there a long time and someone was bound to come looking for them soon. She only had time to pursue one more train of thought.

"What do you do for a living, Claire?"

"I'm a super of this building downtown. I do repair,

maintenance and clean up. Whatever is necessary."

"What would you like to do?"

"It's too late."

"Aw, don't give me that. What would you like to do?"

Claire thought and Ruby waited. Then, just as time was running out, Claire took a chance. "I've always kinda wanted to build houses."

Ruby looked inwardly to that directing wind and thought, okay, it appears this saving will continue, won't it? She felt an answer in the affirmative.

"Well, have I got a house for you! And two guys who can teach you a lot! Call me and come by. Just see what you think!"

Claire took Ruby's card and tucked it carefully away. Then they stood up together. Claire grabbed her arm.

"I'm sorry but I have to ask. Who are you? And why did you come here?"

Ruby laughed, hugged her, took her face in both hands and kissed her on the forehead.

"Isn't it obvious by now? I came here to meet you."

31

CLAIRE AND RUBY WALKED out of the bathroom, holding hands. The bar was more crowded now, but the original eight were still holding fast. The women who had previously applauded now cheered at the sight of Claire looking so good.

Reardon was in a good conversation with the bartender, which was music to Ruby's ears. And speaking of music, she walked over to the karaoke mike.

"Is this on?" she asked. It shrieked in response. Everybody laughed. She went over and adjusted it.

"You know, I haven't done this a lot lately but I really feel like singing something for my new friend, Claire. So I'll just do it with no accompaniment. Is that okay?"

People clapped. She looked inwardly to the winds of

direction that had brought her this far and asked them for a song request. The song they chose surprised her even coming out of her mouth, but once she was into it, she knew it was perfect.

She began to sing the old song "Glory of Love" the way she had heard Bette Midler once sing it—slow, sexy and filled with love from an open heart. Though she saw the irony in singing a song about the wonderful parts of love while she was helping Claire to break free of the love she was feeling, Ruby knew that the greater message was to assure her that love was, indeed, everywhere. It was the hardest thing to hear when you were breaking up, yet it was the only thing that mattered for her to hear. Singing to Claire, she had started off slowly and quietly, signaling to the room that this was all she had in the tank. Then, with every line and every verse, she began to build her power and raise the energy up and up, finally ending on...

"That's the glory of love."

She exploded the beginning of the line and then held the last note and let it quiet down and die out slowly. When she finished, there was no sound.

And then the room erupted. People went nuts. Within the next few minutes, she had met everybody in the whole room as they came up to congratulate her. They bought her drinks, slipped her their cards, asked whether she would do another one.

"Nope, that's it for tonight."

She made sure to end up with Claire. When she got to her, she just held her arms out and Claire rushed into them. As she held her tight, she whispered in her ear.

"That was completely for you. Call me. And Claire, I do need you to believe. This world is going to work out for you. I'm sure of it."

Just then, there was a palpable shift in the bar as she turned to her only enemy in the room. Lauren.

"Okay Miss High and Mighty. You've impressed everyone here. Now I'd like to impress something on you. Step outside."

Now everyone was murmuring excitedly. Ruby saw both Reardon and Claire start to rise. She held up her hand and sat them both down with one stare.

"I'm sorry. Run that by me again. Did you say 'step outside', like in the old Westerns?"

"You heard me, Miss High and Mighty. You got the balls for that?"

"I've got 'em and I'd love to. Oh, but there is one small problem."

With that, Lauren smirked, thinking she was going to try to get out of it.

"If I'm going out there as Miss High and Mighty? I'm always mighty but..."

She grabbed one remaining shot that someone had bought her and downed it.

"There!" she smiled. "Now I'm high too! Let's go do this thing."

As she passed the bouncer who had come since they got there, she said in a loud voice to her, "Don't let anyone come out here. Things could get ugly. Y'all will know pretty quickly how this comes out."

Out they went. The second the door closed behind them, Claire ran over to Reardon. "Oh my God. Laurel likes to fight. Does your friend know how to fight?"

"How should I know?" Reardon said. "I didn't even know she could sing!"

32

———

ONCE OUTSIDE, RUBY GRABBED Lauren's right arm.

"Let's do this around the corner." No more jocularity or compassion in Ruby's voice. Only fury remained.

Immediately around the corner, with Lauren slightly in front of her, Ruby grabbed her right arm in two places and twisted, bringing her knee up at the exact moment for extra torque. She heard a crunch and Lauren sagged. Ruby hoped that this would be enough but could see that Lauren had one more assault left in her, so she grabbed the broken arm and used it to propel her head straight into the side of the building.

Now Lauren was on the ground, seeing stars and about to pass out. Ruby couldn't have that. She reached for the water bottle with the remaining water in it. Crouching down to her level, she threw it in Lauren's face, waking her up.

"Stay awake, goddammit. I'm not through with you yet. Are you awake?"

Lauren nodded.

"Can you hear what I'm saying to you?"

Another nod.

"Good. That's good. Now. You will recover relatively quickly from the damage I've caused you. Although you might have to give up your dream to be an Olympic javelin thrower, but there you go.

"I had to break something on you so that you couldn't spin this story a different way. I want you to live with what you've done, Lauren. You know and I know that you were slowly killing that gentle soul in there. Psychologically beating her to a pulp. You know exactly what I'm saying and you are just despicable enough to not care.

"But I care. I care very much. I want her to call and be in touch with me. That is her decision to make. As is her decision to stay with you or not. If she asks me, I'll tell her to run for the hills, the quickest route from your sorry ass. But she may not ask me, in which case, I'll keep my appraisal of you to myself.

"But know this. There are only two people in that bar that think that you are worth a shit. You and her. If I can, I'm going to encourage her to ask for more out of her life than the likes of you. So you are on borrowed time here. Treat her well. Or leave her be.

"And if I ever hear that anything bad has happened to her, I'm coming for you, you understand? So I want you to try, even at this late date, to change up and become an actual human being and do the right thing. Okay? Okay."

Ruby rose up, but couldn't resist one more parting shot. "I certainly hope that tonight has been interesting enough for you."

And with that, Ruby was gone.

33

_____

THE RIDE HOME FOR the two friends was fairly silent. What was there to say?

Reardon drove while Ruby thought.

Halfway home, Reardon finally spoke.

"You changed the course of two lives in there. I saw you do it. I saw your intention to do it. But I don't know how or why you did it."

Ruby was truthful. "I don't know how or why I did it either."

Reardon waited and then spoke. "Okay. I just have one more question for you."

"Yeah?"

"Where'd you learn to sing like that?"

They laughed on down the road, like the good friends they were.

34

ONCE BACK HOME, RUBY had a whirlwind of emotions. Feeling more settled back within herself, she was a little amazed at what she had done. On the one hand, it was all good. On the other hand, in one short evening, she had gone from compassionately caring someone back to life to taking a seemingly healthy person and breaking her arm!

Had she thought she was capable of that violence? She knew that she had her dad's anger buried deep, something he never showed but was always there. His anger sublimation found a growing host in her, though he would never have guessed that and she too had very seldomly expressed it.

Certainly she could hear Yaron, her martial arts teacher, saying that there was no point in training the way she had trained without acknowledging that she was capable of doing what she had to do in any given situation. That was the goal of the training!

She had never felt such extremes, nor had she ever caused as big a stir as she did tonight. There were several points during the evening when she knew she was ready to do anything. Whatever it took. Her willingness scared the shit out of her at the same time that it was absolutely exhilarating.

She realized, in retrospect, that she could have gotten seriously hurt in that fight but for better or worse, she hadn't even thought about that then. She just had to win.

She proved something to herself with that fight. She knew it wasn't adrenaline that propelled her forward. It was getting backed into a corner and having to keep thinking. Having to stay brave. Keeping the surprise on your side, as Yaron would say over and over again.

She suddenly remembered a guy in LA who was a big playboy. She was drinking with him one night and she asked him what his secret with women was. She was always interested in people's strategies in life. He laughed and explained it to her.

"You really want to know?" She nodded, eagerly.

"Contrary to what you must think, I don't think every woman will go for me. In fact, given enough time to think about it, I wouldn't approach any woman, let alone a woman that I know is beyond my station in life.

"But long ago, the one thing I learned I could count on was my ability to talk myself out of any situation. And believe you me, that ability has been tested countless times and I have always seemed to escape. Some times swimmingly, some times by the short hairs. But I have always survived.

"So you know what I started doing? I started walking up to the most beautiful woman in the room and just planting myself right in front of her. And when she would turn to face me, I would just started talking, to get myself out of it. In the end, the majority of them went out with me."

"Wait a minute. You did that to me!"

"Yep, I did."

"And I saw through your bullshit right away."

"Yep, you did."

"So?"

"So where are we today? And who are you asking advice from?"

Laughing, she said, "Point taken."

About then, they started up a kiss that had lasted about three hours. The man had some skills.

Many years later, tonight, she finally knew what he meant. She had stood with her back to the biggest bully in the room and finessed her way out of it. All of that was the measure of her as a human being.

As a reader of energy, something very different happened tonight. Ruby had help, a director of sorts. She was being used for an end that she couldn't know till she knew it. She was thinking on her feet but she was also being carried.

Claire had needed her help, her specific help. How could Ruby have known that? This night and its story hadn't started or ended with her. She knew that all too well. She had to get to the bottom of it. It was time to get some supplies and then get up on the roof.

She walked into the darkened kitchen and got her bearings. Frank was a stickler about turning lights off, which was a good thing, especially when you equated the cost of the light bill to the number of donuts sold.

Opening the fridge, she pulled out her homemade lemonade, which was getting better and better, due to it being the biggest request from the boys. Then she opened the fridge and got out the bottle of Stoli. Mixing a big drink, she closed everything up and went upstairs to her room.

She put the drink on the roof ledge and went back for two more things. A recently rolled joint went next to the drink.

Then she crept down the hall. Frank was sleeping inside this week as they did some additional repairs on his house out back. She knew that Frank was a very light sleeper but his door was ajar, in case Mutt needed to go out at night.

"Who's there? Is that you, Ruby?"

"Sorry to wake you, Frank. I just needed Mutt."

"Well, here he comes." Mutt bounded out to see her. He had obviously just been dead asleep and he kept shaking his head to wake up. But he was needed and he felt it.

"Goodnight Frank. Hi Buddy!" She petted Mutt.

Together, they went down the hall to her bedroom. Mutt never went out on the ledge with her, which she was glad for. But he could stand or sit right below it, where she could reach back in easily and pet him, which she did as she stepped out onto the roof. She would reach back in from time to time, finding his face and cupping her hand around it. Petting Mutt ranked up there with life's best moments.

When she was on her roof, she could look up and see only endless sky. So it was sky above and humans living below while she hung out in between, surrounded by that magnificent sky and gorgeous land. Years back, when she had first lived in LA in a very tiny apartment, she had looked out the window and talked to her favorite neon sign. Now she was talking to stars.

"Starry, starry nights...," she sang.

Mutt made a little groaning sound. He was happy.

"Starry, starry nights..."

"What a beautiful night! And what a stupid, fucking song."

"Then why do you keep singing it?"

Ruby sat straight up. A voice had answered her. Not a whisper of a voice. Not a possible voice. A flat out voice. In her head. She answered it out loud.

"Who are you? Are you real?"

"You know I'm here. I've always been here."

"This is the first I know of you being here." With every line between them, she was scared that he wouldn't answer again and she was almost as scared that he would.

"Really? First time? How about earlier tonight?" He had said it casually, but she gasped. "Oh my God, was that you?"

"Yeah. That was me. Well, not all me. I just directed things around a little. You did all the heavy lifting."

"What.," she couldn't find the words.

"Congratulations, by the way. I thought you would do well, but I didn't know you'd do that well. You changed the balance tonight. You should be proud of yourself."

"I didn't know what I was doing half the time."

"Yes you did. You knew soon enough."

Everything he was saying was resonating as totally right. At the same time, she wondered if this was what insanity felt like. She could feel his energy-low key, supportive, quiet. She knew she wasn't just having a conversation with herself because the sentences from him were coming out before she could think them.

"What do you call yourself?"

"I don't call myself." And with that, he chuckled.

"I think I'd like to call you Sam."

"Why Sam?"

"Because if this were a movie, I'd want you to be played by Sam Shepard, standing out in a field, gazing meaningfully into the distance."

"Does he do that a lot?"

"Oh yeah, that's one of his best things."

"Then Sam it is. And I am telling you that while staring meaningfully into the distance."

"You catch on quick."

"So do you."

They talked for a bit-enough for her to get her bearings.

Sam advised her to start taking him in, in small doses. He would speak to her from time to time and give her signs. There would never be any pressure for them to talk. In fact, she could choose to never speak to him again and everything would be fine. But if she wanted his input, she could just listen and watch for signs. Ruby's reactions kept ranging from total shock to the feeling that Sam had, indeed, been there for a long time.

This moment and this conversation felt like a culmination

and a beginning, all in one.

"By the way, every moment is like that, you know. A culmination and a beginning, all in one."

Before they ended their first full conversation, he advised her not to think her way into this, just feel and sense it.

"Besides you know, your head and your thoughts aren't the highest part of the food chain like you humans think they are."

"Tell that to my culture. They think thought is everything."

"Yeah, and look where that's gotten them. Sleep well, my friend."

And right there, sitting up on that roof, talking to a spirit and petting her dog, everything had just changed.

35

ODDLY ENOUGH, AFTER EVERYTHING that had happened the night before, Ruby slept better than she could ever remember sleeping.

She woke up late with Mutt sleeping next to her. An irrational happiness spread through her whole body. She wondered if she was just crazed with alcohol and adrenaline and had dreamed the whole night up. Especially Sam.

With a small voice, she asked, "Sam?"

He appeared, smiling, *"I'm here."*

She smiled and went back to sleep.

36

THE MONTHS PASSED HAPPILY. Ruby was getting to be a damned good baker, at least according to Reardon, who was really the only judge that counted. She asked Ruby to make a princess cake for Trudy's seventeenth birthday. It was Trudy's favorite and Reardon made one every year. She could do one in her sleep but she asked Ruby to do it. A princess cake was nothing you could wing. It was either exactly right or it was wrong. She knew Reardon wouldn't let her fail, but Ruby slaved over it. When it was presented and the family pronounced it "perfect," she felt a level of pride she seldom allowed herself to feel.

Ruby and Reardon visited the gay bar several more times, with no huge drama. Though Reardon hadn't hooked up with anybody yet, Ruby could feel her getting more and more comfortable.

According to the bartender, Lauren and Claire had stopped coming in after that night. Ruby felt a bit guilty about that, knowing how few gay bars there were in Madison and knowing that she had burned this one for them.

"Let it go. Detach. You'll understand in due time." Sam had been teaching her about detachment.

Most of the immediate improvements on the house and on Frank's house in back were done. Ruby missed having Frank in the house, but consoled herself by running out every morning with his coffee. She knew that Frank liked this ritual too.

"Frank? Are you decent?" she asked every time she went out there, just to hear him chuckle. She would often see him out on the front stoop, just whittling or looking out. She had begun to realize the beauty of him moving back there; that he needed his solitude as much as she did, which made them the perfect pair. They still ate dinner and played cards most nights.

Maybe I should marry him, she thought to herself, one night over a game of gin rummy with him. It doesn't get a whole lot better than this.

"Yes, it does. It will." Sam was there to quietly remind her. And then just as quickly, he was gone.

She kept thinking about future projects to do with Frank. They were good doing projects together. Some time in the future, he could instruct her on how to plant corn in their field.

That seemed great, but fairly overwhelming. And there was that waterwheel, which they hadn't even spoken about yet.

The barn stood—or sort of stood—as the next big project. But it would have to wait. Daniel was busy, finishing high school and starting to plan his classes at the woodworking school in Wausau after that. She missed him but hoped he was immersed in his friends and his future. If that didn't include as much time at her house, that was probably for the best. Besides, she would see him at graduation in a little over a month. She was going to that graduation to cheer him on as well as to congratulate a couple of her clients who were graduating too.

Though her life was busy and lacked for nothing right now, she knew there was something out there, another mission like the gay bar, either sooner or later. She didn't ask Sam about it, because she knew what he would say. Something to the effect of letting it go till it happens. Some sort of zen thing like that.

"It'll happen when it happens." He chimed into her thoughts.

Sam wasn't above some playful moments, showing off his skills. Once, in the middle of a session, Ruby was having a really hard time penetrating this young girl's defiance. She knew that the girl wanted to break through it and was desperately fighting it as well. Something was really off in her past, but she insisted it wasn't anything she could remember.

One session, as the girl and Ruby kept examining her

life, Sam popped into Ruby's head and said, *"Ask her about her uncle."* This was quite unusual because Sam didn't make a habit of intervening in her sessions, with the exception of her asking him something specific and even then, it wasn't during the session itself. But this one time, she assumed that her level of inner frustration at getting through this hurdle must have summoned him.

"Ask her about her uncle," he repeated.

She sighed. In for a penny, in for a pound, as her relatives used to say.

"Permit me an odd question. Do you have an uncle?"

"Do I have an uncle? No," she said, frustrated. "Jeez, where did that come from?"

Ruby inwardly rolled her eyes at Sam and silently admonished him. "Thanks a lot, big guy."

"Wait for it," he said. And then he was gone.

They began to talk about some other subject when Ruby realized that her client had stopped talking.

"Wait a minute. I know this sounds weird but I did have an uncle. Not an actual uncle but a friend of the family. We called him Uncle Jim."

They sat still for almost fifteen minutes until slowly the defiant mask that the young girl had worn for years began to dissolve. Details of the molestation came out slowly.

37

———

THE LATE SPRING WAS in full bloom. As long as Ruby took her allergy medication, she could and did go running.

It was beautiful to run out along the edges of fields. She loved to stare at crops growing. Up out of this ground, these fields were creating and perpetuating life in its purest form.

On her most energetic days, Ruby would sing out there, into the wind—sometimes running, sometimes pausing. She missed singing and the singer she had become. Was that person left behind in Los Angeles, she wondered. One song at a gay bar does not a singer make! But overcoming her sadness about this was a very solid feeling that the singer in her would come back into play as time went on. She felt certain of it.

One morning, she took off early after baking with Reardon

and began her run from the shop. This time she crossed over the road and into a little group of houses that she had never been by before. Before too long, she hit a dead end and decided to turn and double back to a bigger road when she heard someone yell out.

"HEY!" a voice yelled behind her. She didn't know the voice but knew that the "hey" was aimed straight at her—and held fury.

"Never shied away yet," she muttered, reminding herself of an old internal martial arts motivating phrase she used to utter. Taking a deep breath, she turned to face the fury.

"Yes, you!" The voice was coming from a woman, who was walking towards her in a housecoat, her face twisted in rage.

"You counsel a girl named Deborah, don't you?"

Ruby didn't answer. She didn't tell anyone the names of her clients.

"Well get this! I'm her damned mother. That's who I am."

Still two feet away, Ruby could already smell the alcohol wafting off of this woman. Deborah had told her extensively about her mother's alcoholism and here, in the morning, was the proof. The smell was very distinctive to Ruby. It was the smell of alcohol coming out of the woman's pores, signifying that she was never without that smell. It was the smell of someone pickling their insides.

She remembered an alcoholic teacher of hers in LA. He

always showed up to class with a freshly starched shirt and wet, clean hair, but the pickling smell was always there. After a point, it couldn't be washed away.

Now the woman was yelling again. Ruby winced at the sound, but knew there was no point in trying to quiet her down. This scene was going to happen.

"Because of you, the light of my life won't talk to me anymore. And why? Because she'd rather talk to you! Oh God."

The combination of the woman's disgust and the alcohol made her start to reel a bit.

"Why don't you just get your own daughter, 'stead of taking mine, you child stealer!"

She spat on the ground. Ruby had the distinct feeling that she had planned to spit on her, but it was too bright out and she couldn't lift her head up that far.

"She works longer at her job so she can pay to talk to you rather than talking to me for free! Do you believe that?"

Now the woman was very close to her. Ruby could barely breathe now from the up close smell of how loaded she was. But she also knew from Deborah that this woman, her mom, had lost her oldest child, a son, in Iraq. Her grief was real. It was earned. Despite the last few minutes, her heart went out to her.

"I'm sorry. I do hope that things between you two can get stronger."

"You could make that happen, you know. By just going away!"

Ruby knew this wasn't true. This woman had no way to face the fact that she had lost her daughter's trust and admiration years ago.

"That is Deborah's call and hers alone. If she wants to get closer to you, I will support her in that."

The woman tried to grasp some kind of victory from Ruby's words. "Well, that's at least something."

Ruby knew she had to say the rest of it, knowing that she would be hurting this woman even more. But saying just the first half would be wrong.

"But I will support her in whatever she chooses to do. These aren't yours or my choices to make, they are hers alone and I will support her in making them."

With that she turned around and began to slowly walk away.

"Whore. CHILD STEALER!" And with that, one more spit.

Wow, Ruby thought, not turning back around. And you wonder where your child's admiration went? But that was too easy a retort and she knew it. She also knew she was spooked. Though this woman and her grief had isolated her from everyone, could she run Ruby out of town? The whole incident preyed on some ancient fears she realized she had.

Once home, she went up and onto the roof, hoping that

Sam would be there and knowing that he would be because she needed him.

"Was it me? Did I cause that interaction?" she asked the sky, expecting no answer.

Sam appeared in her head.

"You caused it. And you didn't cause it. You are a part of it and it would have happened without you."

"Great. Huh? So what are you telling me?"

"Cease and desist from holding only one truth in your head. You are important and change everything around you. And you aren't important at all. You are to blame for your actions and there is no such thing as blame."

"How does this help me out?"

Sam laughed softly. *"It doesn't. It makes things a lot more complicated. But it gets you a whole lot closer to the truth."*

"Couldn't you help me a little bit?"

"I am helping you. Accept the paradox. Have faith."

"Faith in...?"

"Faith that there are way too many people who like and love you for you ever to be run out oftown. Faith that you have all that you need to handle anything in this one moment. And faith to remember that this one moment is all that there is."

Ruby smiled. "Moment to moment then, Sam?"

"Moment to moment, life is always fresh and new."

38

HIGH SCHOOL WAS DONE. Graduation day rolled around. Ruby and Frank got ready to go to the afternoon ceremony. Ruby assumed that Daniel would think they would come, but she hadn't seen him recently at any point to tell him for certain that they would be there.

As they sat down on the bleachers, Ruby surveyed the students. She immediately saw her two graduating senior girls, giggling and looking proud at the same time. She scanned for Daniel. He was further back, due to his height.

As she looked at him, she saw his point about being older than the other kids. But it wasn't only that. He wasn't a part of them. As she looked at him, she realized that she was looking at a real man, who was sitting in the middle of a lot of kids.

As she continued to stare, a gold light seemed to come up behind him, emanating from all around him. She was sure she was seeing things, but she had to ask.

"Nice light show, Sam," she said internally.

"Pretty, isn't it?"

"So you made it?"

"Nah. I see it but I didn't make it. You did."

As soon as she heard that, the light was gone.

Later, as graduates and their families and friends mingled, Daniel came up to Ruby and Frank, hugging them each in a perfunctory way. She wondered why he seemed to be holding them at a distance, but there wasn't time to ponder this now.

"Congrats, Daniel. I have a little present for you, but I left it on the table at home."

"No matter, Ruby. Hang on to it. I'll be over soon."

At that point, some giggly girls came over to flirt with him. He introduced them and then added, "A bunch of us are going out for pizza. Thanks for being here today, both of you." And with that, he allowed himself to be whisked away.

In order not to show the confusion this was bringing up in her, she turned quickly to Frank with a mock dramatic voice and said, "Oh Frank! Our little boy is all grown up!"

He laughed and they went back home.

39

AT HOME AND EARLIER to bed than usual, Ruby toyed with the idea of pouring a bucket of cold water on herself. It was now alarmingly clear to her that her passion for Daniel was out of control.

She hadn't done much on the sexual front since she moved here, now over a year ago. A few dalliances with some men in Milwaukee were fun but nothing that really ignited her passion. Just some fun sex and thanks a lot, see you around. That type of thing.

But now and, as Riley had said, without negotiation, her body was aching for this man. Who cares how old he is anyway? He could be in fucking preschool and if he looks like that...

She couldn't imagine him having fun having pizza with

those girls. Though she knew she had to be able to imagine it. How else could she begin to move on?

She must have dozed off because she woke with a start at the sound of the front door being opened. She looked around for a weapon to use, but there was nothing around since this had never been a remote problem before and she hadn't even thought of it.

But wait, she reasoned, there was no sound of forcing the door open. It just opened and closed. It must be Frank! That's it. He was the only one with a key! Except that time when she had given a key to Daniel.

The door to her room opened and Daniel stood there.

His white shirt was already unbuttoned. His face wasn't light in anyway. The passion she had been feeling was clear, all over him.

With a predatory smile that had no humor in it, just sexual acquisition, he said, "I came for my graduation present."

Trying desperately to diffuse the situation so she could think, she stood up quickly and said, "Oh, it's down on the kitchen table."

"No it isn't. We both know that."

And with that, he strode right up to her and stopped just short of touching her. She couldn't stand it. They came together after months and months of longing. Kissing, tearing off each other's clothes, sucking, touching, pulling hair, diving into each other.

Then he did something that thrilled her even more. He picked her up and threw her on the bed.

And, in the carnality of it all, she lost her mind.

He was on her and in her, driving further and further into her, kissing and exploring every inch of her...

And she just wanted more! She wanted every inch of this man, from head to toe. To kiss him, to lick him, to be penetrated by him. The fear that she had all along had come true. Once inside her, she knew she would never get enough, that she would want him more. And more. And more....

Hours later, after she ran and got them both some water, they allowed themselves a little time to talk.

She sat down on the bed and allowed herself the sensation of looking at him without touching him. It felt like exquisite torture. All that sweaty, tanned, muscled skin... she laughed for a moment and smiled at him.

"Nice little staging with the girls and the pizza."

"You liked that, huh?"

"Frustrated me no end."

"Good! That's what it was supposed to do."

"Well, you little player! Did you even go out with them?"

"First off, can you stop referring to me as little?"

"I'm thinking that after tonight, I'm going to have to."

"And no. Duh! What do you take me for? How could I hang out with those nut jobs when I've had you."

"But you hadn't had me yet."

"That's what you think, lady. I happen to possess a very active imagination. You have already been pummeled 50 ways from Friday. Some of them have been quite imaginative."

"Gee, maybe you'd like to elaborate? Revisit them?"

His dick was hard and moving back up her thigh. "No time like the present."

She felt herself sinking back into him and their sexual bliss.

"No time at all."

40

———

THE WEEKS THAT FOLLOWED for Ruby were filled with Daniel and ridiculous amounts of sex. Their only shared worry was about Frank's feelings if he found out. They agreed that they would accept whatever he thought or felt, but they weren't quite ready to find out yet. So they tried not to be together around him. This led to sex in the fields, in the car, in the lake, in a canoe (not successful but fun to try) and almost every night, Daniel slipped into Ruby's bed for several hours.

Neither one of them could get enough. If he was late to come over, she was moaning by the time he got there.

"My God, you're hot. Can't you just calm down a little?"

"Yeah, you know I've tried! But apparently not," she said, truthfully.

"Well good. Keep it turned up. Wouldn't want it any other way."

They tried being together in public places, like an ice cream parlor or a convenience store, and not touching each other. It was almost impossible. They would finish their cones and run around to the back of the building, with a buildup of passion that had to be quenched.

One night, Frank and Ruby were having dinner alone together. Frank asked her a question.

"Why don't we have Daniel for dinner anymore?"

Ruby was blindsided. "I don't know."

"You two are making each other very happy, so I think he should be able to show his face at dinner."

"How did you know?"

Frank looked at her. "Have you seen your face lately?" He chuckled at that. "The way you walk and talk? Look in the mirror!

"It wasn't hard to figure out who was making you so happy. I've been around you both for a good while and saw the looks you gave each other. At first, I thought it was all coming from him to you. But then I started watching you. I may be seventy, but I know those looks!" And with that, he shook his head, smiling.

"Oh Frank, do you think I'm terrible? I'm a decade older than him."

"Which will matter less with every passing year. Oh, I admit, I was worried for both of you at the start. But it seems to be working like a charm right now. So enjoy this and take care of the future when it comes."

"What if people start talking about us? What will they say?"

He laughed. "What's that song you love? The James Hunter one?"

Now she laughed. "People Gonna Talk." She knew that just by saying it, she had just queued up that song for her mental loop for the rest of the night.

"Well you know they will talk. But you've never seemed like a gal to let that curb her actions. Besides, the ones that care about you will take their cue from you."

In a flash, she realized that those were her exact words to Reardon about her kids' reactions to her choices.

Very seriously, Frank reached over and patted her hand. "I'm happy for you, my girl."

Ruby saw his fatigue. He was a man of few words and that had been a lot for him.

"Thank you Frank. Truly. And hey, maybe there's a sixty to eighty year-old woman out there for you!"

"Well, let's find her and get this ball rolling!"

They laughed but she knew Frank was just kidding her,

to make her feel in good company. He would never look at another woman. Frank was still married to Clara and he always would be.

41

AS THE SUMMER WANED, things started to get into a more normal rhythm. Daniel was starting classes in Wausau soon, as well as apprenticing several days a week with a nearby carpenter.

Ruby was quite busy as well. Reardon was having some foot trouble with her bunions, but the doctor had given her corrective socks and shoes and said she might be able to avoid surgery if she stayed off her feet and rested them every couple of hours. So Ruby stepped up to help her friend during this time, moving easily but tiredly into more hours and even acting as the lead baker on days when Reardon couldn't stand anymore. That meant she saw her clients in the afternoons and evenings, which was fine. But exhaustion meant early nights. Not exactly uneventful early nights when Daniel was around, but early nights, nonetheless.

Sam dropped in from time to time giving her some important energetic lessons, always offhandedly and yet always with deep import.

He taught her a bit more about how to read energy, all the different energies there were and how to interpret the psychic "hits" that she had so naturally always gotten off of people. She was always grateful for his help in refining her energetic boundaries and awareness.

Ruby keenly sensed that there were adventures ahead, but that Sam was building her up methodically till he knew what she was capable of.

And then, in one moment, everything changed.

It was a night when Ruby was experimenting in the kitchen by making a savory pie for her and Frank. She had the tiny TV on, which was unusual. They seldom used it, each preferring silence and the sounds of nature.

Ruby was only sort of half watching the news. The news program was ending with a story about the mysterious death of a vintner in Sonoma, California.

"Cause of death is still unknown, though police suspect foul play. Services are to be held..."

Ruby was still only listening with half an ear to the story until Sam stopped her cold in her tracks with one sentence.

"You know, you could help with that situation. Are you game?"

The time she had always known would come had just arrived.

42

———

DRIVING TO MILWAUKEE, RUBY had no real ideas for how to pull off the first step of her multi-step plan. Come to think of it, she had no idea what the rest of the steps were either, though she knew they would appear in due time.

Step one was clear but tough to contemplate doing. She needed to tell Shelby and Riley all about Sam. It was a subject that she hadn't ever brought up with them. In fact, up until this situation, she wasn't sure that she ever would. Sam, and the adventures of Sam, didn't seem to fall into their wheelhouse. More than a little apprehensive, she couldn't see another way. She would either hit a wall or move through this. Tonight would be the defining moment in whether or not there was even a chance for her to take this trip.

Settled into Riley's sofa and two bottles of wine later, she had told them both about Sam, relaying everything she could think of to tell them about him, up to the present moment. Then she held her breath for their reactions.

Shelby got the awkwardness, so she spoke first. "I always thought you were a little cagey about that gay bar story. Felt like you were leaving something out. That's why I had you tell it to me a couple of times."

Riley cast Shelby a disapproving glance. "Oh, so that's why? So you say." Then, just as quickly, he dismissed it and was on to something else. "And how pray tell, my little bun maker, are you supposed to know what to do once you get there?"

"Watch and listen, he says." Ruby answered.

"Now Riley," Shelby reasoned, as she stroked Riley's arm, "just because you and I have not had the "gift" bestowed upon us of a special communication, such as this, does not mean it doesn't make a lot of sense. Look at the other experiences she described where he was driving the bus. They've worked out well."

"I suppose. Well, it sounds entertaining, to say the least."

"Sam says the Sonoma adventure will appeal to my love for travel and my affinity for grapes," Ruby chuckled.

"He's got that right. Say! It's like he's in your head or something!"

"Riley G," Shelby warned, trying to pull him back.

"I don't expect you to believe me," Ruby told him.

"Yeah and I don't," he snapped. "But no matter.

"I'm sorry, honey. You are about as sane as any I've run across in this world. And if you believe what you're saying, you are either insane—but still delightful—or you have seen something that I haven't seen. And God knows, with the amount of time I spend up in here, there is a good deal I won't be seeing...Oh, and as per that, I couldn't be happier about it."

His flourish made them all laugh. Then his mood turned on a dime and he got serious.

"Here's the thing. I'm going to be paying for this trip," he interrupted Ruby's potential interruption with one of his silencing hard stares.

"First of all, if I don't, Shell here will hound me to the gates of hell..."

"Absa-fucking-lutely!" Shelby interjected in triumph.

"...and second, even if I don't believe it and currently see you as sort of a whack job, you are nevertheless my friend the whack job and I decree that you need a serious romp. Just remember, I require a good story out of it. That's all. But sordid details will be required."

Ruby allowed herself a smile at this. "You know, it's funny. I always thought about going up there to Sonoma when I lived in

LA, but I never did. Napa a few times, but never to Sonoma. But Riley, are you sure about the money?"

"Oh honey, you know I'm rolling in it. And God knows there will be a good story at the end. Besides, I'm gay. Who else am I gonna shower my money on? I mean, other than two-bit whores..."

Shelby laughed. "Well at least they only cost two bits."

"Oh don't kid yourself honey. That's the pathetic part. They cost far more than they're worth."

"And they're still worth two bits!" they said together and started to laugh and laugh.

Ruby nestled back, to the sound of their patter that she loved so much.

After Shelby went home early, Riley got her a first class ticket leaving in two days and a rental car when she got into San Francisco. She kissed him and said she'd pay him back.

"Don't you dare," he said. "A good story is all I require."

When she got to the car and reached in her bag for her keys, there was one thousand dollars in hundreds stuffed inside.

43

___

THERE WAS ONLY ONE obstacle left, but it wasn't a small one. She would tell Daniel as much as she could without mentioning Sam. She needed time for that.

It was funny. Once Sam had started to talk with her, she asked him if she could tell people about him. He kept saying it would take more time than she thought to tell people. And, like everything he casually popped up and said, it turned out to be true.

In a way, Riley and Shelby had been the easiest to tell. Both majored in strange in their lives, so their strange tolerance was pretty high.

Nobody majored in strange in Rural. Reardon's gayness, for instance, was the furthest out point on the pendulum for the two of them to discuss; whereas with Riley, it was the starting point. In legal circles, he flew under cover effortlessly. But if you knew him, that was just where the truth started. And then, if he felt like telling stories—which you wanted him to do because he was the world's best storyteller—you got to hear all about strange! All kinds of strange. Riley was fascinated by strange.

Ruby worried that, as effortlessly as her conversation with Sam had started, it would change how people saw her and she wasn't in a hurry for that.

With Daniel, it was never a question that she would eventually tell him about Sam. She thought about it often. It was just that she didn't want to lose the exact relationship they were having right now. Not even by a bit.

And yet here she was, about to risk it. She needed the air to be clear.

Lying in bed with her, Daniel said, "So, I see your suitcase is out. Where are you going?"

"Daniel, I need to tell you. And I need to tell you in small doses. For me, not for you. Oh man, I'm blowing this! Okay. From time to time, I might go away—or I'm going to be going away for short periods of time—because someone needs my help. I promise, I will make all of this make more sense as soon as I can.

"Here's the thing. I don't know in advance what I'll have to do. But if I can heal a situation, I'm going to do it. I need to be free to do that."

She stopped. Daniel thought about it for a couple of minutes. Ruby realized she was holding her breath. How could he begin to understand the weird thing she was telling him without knowing all of it? Yet, it suddenly seemed incredibly important to see if he could live with just the amount of information she was giving him. For now. After several moments of silence, he spoke.

"Do you think these trips and what you have to do will affect us?"

"No. I will do everything in my power not to jeopardize anything between us. You are too magical to lose."

After some more thought, he spoke slowly and quietly, "Ruby, you are my absolute dream woman. You have all the qualities I could ever want. You are a crazy woman in bed, you cuss like a sailor and you fill my life so far up—like I never imagined it could be filled. So yeah. I'll trust you. I'll take whatever amount of you I can get."

"You are quite an amazing man."

"Don't laugh at this, but...you've made me that man, Ruby. A man that can handle you." The kiss that followed was full of love and acceptance from both of them.

"Now. If you just won't feel the need to 'heal' a lot of guys in Rural, I'd appreciate it." They laughed and punched each other, starting to wrestle. "Can you imagine?!" They both squealed.

Later, she said, "There's a lot you don't know about me yet."

He turned to her. "I know what I need to know." His hand slowly moved down between her legs. "And when I need to find out more, I'll torture the rest out of you."

She gasped.

44

———

"YOU RENTED ME A Beemer?" Ruby said to Riley. She was driving from San Francisco towards Napa, using the hands-free phone.

"Why not? It's the car I drive. Besides, I can't have my girl out there spiritually healing from a Buick. Just doesn't conjure the shit right."

After they hung up, Ruby blasted her music. She'd made a handful of CDs, bringing some serious tunage with her and relishing a nice, long drive with the singers she loved.

Hard not to love looking at this California scenery, she thought. There were cows, like back home, and all these ridiculously gorgeous vines. This time in the late summer had to be the greatest time to drive through them. The grapes were hanging down below the leaves, full and almost ready to pick. They hadn't been harvested yet but were practically bursting on the vine.

Her drive was going well. Maybe a bit too well. She looked up and saw that she was deep in the heart of Napa, almost to St. Helena.

"Oh God, I completely forgot to turn to Sonoma! What am I doing Sam? Am I lost?"

"This looks alright," was all she got back.

She slowed down, looking at the little B&B's she was passing by. She was mentally organizing how to turn around and get back to Sonoma, when a sign caught her eye:

THE SHADY PINES HOUSE

This seemed rather amusing to her, especially since the house didn't seem particularly shady and there were no pine trees on it. But it was the sign directly below that made her gasp a little. Hanging down, it said:

MUTTS - WELCOMED & LOVED!

Just keep following the signs...

She stopped the car and went in.

45

RUBY STEPPED INSIDE, ADJUSTING her eyes to the darker room. Immediately she was greeted by an extremely large woman. She had big eyes, a wide, lovely smile and a sweatshirt that would have put her in the same club as Dot back home.

"Hi, I'm Margie! Nice to meet you! You made it just in time for tea. Can I make you some? Or would you prefer some wine?"

"Whatever you're having is fine."

"I could go either way!"

"Okay, let's do some wine."

"You got it!"

As Margie prepared the wine in the kitchen, Ruby thought she was in the right place. The sign out front seemed to say it all. But what if she wasn't and she was in the wrong place? Had she picked up on the wrong sign? Watch and listen...

"So," she said loud enough for Margie to hear, "You are obviously a dog-friendly place? That's great. I love my dog."

"Oh yes, I just never could resist 'em. And people have really only brought great dogs here," she said, coming in with a tray, a bottle of wine, two glasses and a cheese plate.

"So, if you love dogs, would you like to meet mine?"

"Oh definitely," Ruby said, taking a sip of wine as Margie turned away to call her dog.

"Riley? Come in here and meet this nice lady!"

With her back turned away towards her dog, Margie missed Ruby's spit take, but thought she heard something, so turned back.

"Everything all right dear?"

"Um, yes! Sure. Sorry about that. Say, I wonder, do you have a room for me for the next couple of nights?"

46

WHEN RUBY CRAWLED in bed that night, she missed Daniel. Not only the sex but how much fun they had with each other. She hadn't allowed herself to know him too well till they got together, but now that she had, she never could have guessed how easy they would be with each other.

She knew she brought out the playfulness in him. One night, she was telling him about having to perform Shakespearean monologues in acting class in LA. That was all well and good, but any fool could see she had no chance of being any good as King Henry the Fifth leading his men into battle.

"I mean, who's gonna buy me saying 'Once more unto the breach, dear friends, once more, or close the wall up with our English dead'!"

She had never seen Daniel laugh that hard about anything. He made her say it over and over, using an affected British accent, and he would just double over. One day, after a particularly physical afternoon with him, she was standing by her window naked. He walked up behind her and recited the two lines over and over as he fucked her.

Later she said, "Congratulations, by the way. You've just superseded every dismal association I have with that King Henry material." From then on, it was one of their many code words for initiating sex. He would walk in after work, sit down and chat until one of them would say, oh so casually, "once more unto the breach dear friends, once more?" To which the other would say, "or close the wall up with our English dead!" And just like that, off they would walk. And then run.

Riley was right. Sex—and true happiness-required no negotiation.

She awoke in Napa, feeling very alive. This trip was already agreeing with her. She loved the fly- by-the-seat-of-your-pants aspect to it. Deciding that she too would call the trip a happy one if she had at least one good story to tell Riley and Shelby, she felt confident. That seemed extremely doable.

As she came down the stairs to breakfast, something smelled divine. "Wow, Margie, what have you whipped up for us?"

"Well, first we have a baked apple with caramel infused

clotted cream. And after that, my double thick lemon pancakes with local butter and syrup!"

Since working at the bakery, Ruby had been following Reardon's example of not eating too much sugar early in the morning. She had coffee when she was at the bakery and one donut or slice of something yummy around midday. That way, her blood sugar would stay even while she was making all of the orders. But today? Not a chance! It looked great and she wasn't exactly being offered any healthy choices.

Glancing around at the four other people already eating in the room, she smiled, made eye contact and said "hi." They seemed oblivious and not friendly.

Ruby sat down and had a few bites of everything, trying to beg off eating more. She told Margie how good it all was. Looking down at Margie's bulging ankles, she worried about her heart and these meals, but didn't feel like she could mention anything. Besides, if she was supposed to, the space and the opportunity would open for it to happen.

Yeah! she thought happily. I think I'm starting to get the hang of this!

Riley trotted in and Ruby laughed all over again.

47

RUBY KNEW THE ONE place she needed to aim for—Daninger Wineries. It was Mr. Daninger who was killed, and if she could help in Sonoma at all, it was probably something around that death. Wasn't it? Well, that was her first stop anyway. But before that even happened, she probably needed to get her ass over to Sonoma!

Grabbing her map, she said so long to Margie. Told her that she wanted to hear more of her life story later and that she would be back. Margie looked anxious. Ruby realized then how much Margie needed to talk. There were all kinds of loneliness in this world.

It was a bit tricky to find Sonoma. Ruby had traveled to many spots in the world, but always as the queen of alternative transportation-boarding and catching every kind. But driving herself places? As Riley would say, not so much!

However, the drive was beautiful. She made it to the square in the middle of Sonoma and realized what the hoopla was all about. While all of the little towns in Napa were nestled along Highway 29 and catered almost exclusively to the tourists, Sonoma obviously had its own life.

She walked around the square slowly, just getting her bearings. Clearly Sonoma was crawling with tourists. She got a kick out of the fact that it was so obvious who the tourists were and who the locals were. The tourists were wearing filmy, short party dresses and stiletto heels as they traversed very uneven street surfaces. Whereas the locals were comfortable, looking sorta like prosperous former deadheads in comfortable shoes. She would have loved to be a part of this place.

Feeling like walking a bit more after a travel day on the plane, she walked out from the square in several directions. There was a high school ball field one way, reminding her of graduation day. Uh-oh. Better not think about that too much. She could end up accosting a tourist and giving them a day to remember.

Another way took her to a beautiful winery and its grounds. It had obviously been built up as a tourist destination and judging from all the tourists there, the PR was working.

Ruby left there quickly. She didn't like a lot of tourists. Even when she scraped money together to travel the world while she was living in LA, she always went during the rainy season or something like that, so that she would have fewer tourists to deal with. She liked to enter and observe a place quietly.

Dropping down a few blocks, she found a beautiful one hundred-year-old building that was now a Community Center. Grateful for a break from the heat, she stepped inside and walked around. The doors were open to an old restored auditorium. She wondered what went on in there and imagined singing on its high stage.

No sooner had she thought that than she heard faint singing coming from down the hall. Shortly after, a woman came out of the singing room with an adult student. They were laughing and hugging. Then they both talked a bit with the next student who had just arrived. Seemed like one big happy singing family.

Ruby locked eyes with the teacher for a moment. She found someone there she would like to know, but knew that this was not the reason that she was here, so she turned to go.

The teacher had some powers of observation too, and she called out after her.

"Excuse me!"

"Yes?" Ruby said, turning around.

"Do you sing?" she asked, down the hall.

"Yeah, I do."

"Thought so. Come back some time."

Ruby knew that somehow the woman was an energetic peer. The woman had seen into her, as Ruby could as well, in a really beautiful way. She loved that.

"You know what? I hope I do. I'd love to."

With that, they smiled at each other and Ruby headed back towards the square. The city tour had been a nice diversion but now she had work to do.

48

BACK IN THE SQUARE at the town's center, Ruby sat down on a bench for a moment, watching some ducks in the pond. She watched and listened. She knew she could head right to the winery, but sensed that there was some information she needed first.

By the by, two women stopped in front of her. They weren't sort of near her, but right in front of her, just inches away, like she wasn't even there! Okay. Weird. Their bags smelled of rich leather, which reminded her of her Wisconsin cows, particularly the ones she talked to every day on her field runs.

These women were obnoxious and she would have moved away except...probably a sign. She waited. If she had moved an inch, they would realize she was there and leave.

"Aren't there some cute little shops here? So cute!"

"Yeah, totally cute! I knew it would be cute. See?! I told you!"

"You were right, Sonya!"

Since Ruby was invisible anyway, she rolled her eyes freely.

"But the best place so far was that leather shop."

"Oh, I know! And that cute little woman who runs it. I don't think she even knows how good her stuff is!"

And with that, they abruptly moved on. It was almost artificial, like they were in a play and needed to move to their next mark. The weirdness of that scene and their movements told Ruby that she needed to find the leather shop. One of the women had tilted her head in a certain direction when she had spoken of it. Ruby crossed the street, finding it immediately.

To say the shop was small was an understatement. You could walk in straight forward but it was a bit easier to walk in sideways. Though you really didn't have to, something made you duck your head. Inside, the store was packed with all things leather. The smell was intoxicating.

The little woman in question stepped out of the back room. With gray hair and the wisest eyes Ruby had come across in a long time, she felt received before anything was said.

"Welcome. You've come a long way, haven't you?" the woman said with kindness.

Ruby smiled and considered the comment. "Yeah, I think

you'd be right in saying that. But I'm glad to be here."

"Good. That is good," she nodded, with a strong accent.

"Dutch?" Ruby asked.

The woman smiled, as if she had passed a test of some kind.

"Impressive! You are right."

"Not that impressive! Just a guess." Ruby demurred.

"Well then, an impressive guess." The woman was determined to make Ruby feel at home, something she appreciated.

They began to talk in earnest. Jessica was the woman's name and she had lived all over the world. She explained a lot about leather that Ruby didn't know, like the fact that no animals were killed for leather. They always used hides that were collected after the animal was killed for other purposes.

They spoke of Amsterdam, where Jessica had lived and Ruby had visited. Ruby told Jessica her favorite traveling story about Amsterdam. One time, she wasn't really aiming to visit there but simply had a stopover for several hours. Not sure what to do with that short a time, she got a locker to put her stuff in and hopped aboard one of those boats for a tour of the canals.

The boat had a voice over recording that spoke as they glided along. At one point, these two beautiful women were crossing the bridge that the boat was about to go under. The women were nestled together as they walked, obviously a couple.

Just then, the voice over intoned, "Amsterdam has long been protected by its dykes."

With that, they both erupted in laughter. As can only happen on trips, Ruby was happy to have instantly made a friend. If nothing else, she was glad to have come, if only to meet Jessica. This woman was a keeper.

She hit upon an idea and told her about Daniel, who was going to woodworking school. She described him as young and very dedicated and told her how he had helped to fix up her house. She described his deep love of his tools and how he kept buying more—a different sized chisel, a cross-cut saw...But still, could she get one of these leather bags altered with some loops inside to carry at least some of the tools? The tools needed for a specific job, maybe?

Jessica seized on it right away. "We make everything to specification. So let's see what we might want." She immediately opened a bag—the one Ruby was most drawn to—and looked at the inside, then grabbed a pad and started to draw a few ideas. It was so exciting! They made arrangements for it to be sent when it was done.

"Is he a special friend?" Jessica asked, mischievously.

Ruby grinned. "Yeah, special. But young." Why had she voiced that to this new friend, she wondered.

Jessica nodded nonchalantly. "Ah yes, young. But special is

more important than young, don't you think?"

"As a friend of mine likes to say, you've been reading all my mail!" They laughed again.

As Jessica wrote the order up, Ruby took the chance she had originally come in for.

"Have you been reading about that murder at the winery? I heard something about it on the news."

"I haven't been reading about it. But that's mostly because I just hear about it all the time. News passes faster to me by mouths. By the time it's in the paper, it's already old news to me!"

After a slight pause, she continued. "Mr. Daninger was a great man. Everybody liked him. He was a pioneer in these parts; one of the first guys to farm his grapes organically.

"He has four kids and they all work there, as well as two of their spouses."

Ruby wondered. "That all sounds great. Why do they suspect foul play?"

"A couple of reasons. The organic farming came out of his being a health nut. No one can remember him ever being sick a day in his life. If Mr. D had some huge disease, believe me, someone would have known about it."

"And if someone would have known about it, you would already have heard about it!"

Jessica laughed. "You're catching on pretty quick there, my friend!

"But also, the stranger part of it were the rumors that he was thinking about selling out to a larger group of investors, going corporate. No one could imagine that he would do that. He was always so proud of the fact that, while most other smaller wineries that made good sold out, he was one of few independents that had stayed that way."

"Was the winery doing well?"

"Very well. Money rolling in. Lots of articles about his farming techniques. Only thing I can think of is that he wasn't supposed to be a very good bookkeeper. His mother was a top accountant and when she retired, she only worked on his books alone. But she died about three years back and the family took over the accounts. That could have been a problem."

"How did the kids take that possibility of him selling out to a larger group?"

"They put a brave face on it, but you knew they were spooked. They've grown up in wealth and their lives and jobs were set for life. If a corporation took over, how long would some of them get to keep those cushy jobs?"

"Good point. This is so fascinating. I hope you don't mind telling me about this."

"Not at all. I am in possession of so much useless

information, it is a pleasure to give some of it away!"

"I assume you know all of the kids. Do you like them?"

Jessica gave the question serious thought. "They are okay. There is only one gem in the bunch. The oldest daughter, Lisa. She's the real deal. She loved her father and she loves the business. He was giving her more responsibility all the time because she was coming up with so many great ideas. I think she would have eventually taken over the business. But she has one huge downfall."

"Uh-oh. Too bad there always has to be one of those. What was it?"

"She has an absolute loser of a husband. No one in town will tell you that because they think he is too important to be truthful about. But he is all over town, throwing his weight around, openly flirting with every woman, getting drunk and buying everyone a drink, acting like he is going to take over the business.

"Lisa loves him and she doesn't see any of that. In fact, she would seemingly be contented to run the business and let him be the figurehead. Mr. Daninger had seen that and was not happy about it. Such a smart woman she is and yet so blind to this man."

"Hard to imagine that a woman that bright would be taken in like that. But then again, it has happened throughout history," Ruby commented.

"Okay Jessica. You've said enough. You have whetted my appetite. Now I have to go see this place. How do I get there?"

Jessica gave her directions. "Let me know what you thought after you go, if you have a chance."

"You'll be the first to know if I pick up on anything. Although you seem to have it all covered!"

She pulled out her wallet to pay for the bag. She knew it was going to be expensive, somewhere around $400, but well worth it. When she looked down at the bill, it was under $200. When she looked up, Jessica was smiling.

"Hey, wait a minute. This isn't right."

"It is right. There is a friend's discount on there."

"But..."

"Now, you aren't going to insult me and say we aren't friends, are you?"

A look went between the women. The bond between them was formed and very real. She wished for a moment that she could live here and spend much more time with this woman.

"We are friends. You are right about that. Thank you so much."

"Now go. Drink some wine! I have a feeling about you. You're going to advance this story. Report back."

49

DANINGER'S WINERY SAT OFF of Highway 12, at the top of a hill, with a view that went for miles. This whole city specializes in views, Ruby noticed. To get there, you took a windy road that wasn't paved but well kept up.

Walking in, a large bar was in the middle of the space, with artwork all around. There were also a lot of very high end wine products and books at different cluster points in the room. Without having gone to any of the other wineries yet, Ruby still knew she was at a high end one, due to the product lines they had and the beautiful building they were in.

The bar was surrounded by tourists, about two to three layers deep, doing tastings. She despaired about how crowded it was and how she was ever going to find out anything if she was that far back.

Just then a chair at the bar opened up. Ruby didn't rush for it, thinking it was probably rude if there were others waiting. But no one seemed to take it! She waited another couple of minutes and it stayed open.

"Nice move," she said, internally to Sam. "Now you're just showing off!" She felt a distant smile meet her halfway.

Seating herself, a portly young guy came over to her, a bit stressed. He hurriedly told her there were three tasting menus she could purchase, one with whites, one with reds and one with everything.

"The only thing we don't have today is the Chardonnay but we are substituting another Sauvignon Blanc and our newest dry Rose," he said, reciting the disclaimer he had clearly been saying to customers for hours. For Ruby, this presented not an irritant but instead an extra wine to taste so that she could sit and absorb for that much longer.

"Well, I just got to town so let's shoot the moon. I'll take it all."

"Suit yourself!" the guy said. He was too busy to think straight but rang her up. Luckily for her, by taking her time to taste each one, she got a chance to be waited on by all four people pouring. They did a sort of tag team thing, picking up on whoever was ready for the next wine. They would describe it and then pour and leave you alone for a bit to try it.

In the long time that she sat there, people came and went and she watched and listened. She quickly picked up on what had to be the hardest part of the wine pourer's job. Without a doubt, it was to watch all the men that came in with their girlfriends. They would go into lengthy descriptions of each wine to impress their dates, as if they had even the slightest idea of what they were talking about. The pourers had to just stand there and pretend that these guys were filled with insights. It wouldn't do to correct these blowhards if they wanted to end up with a sale.

One guy loudly stated he wanted to bring a large group with him back from the "City" on Sunday. He clearly looked like he was waiting for applause.

"Nope," the guy waiting on them said. "We're closed on Sunday."

"Well, that's unfortunate! Seems like a funny business to be closed on Sundays."

"We don't ordinarily close on Sundays, just this one. It is— or was—Bob, the owner. It's his memorial this Sunday."

Ruby made a mental note of that. It was Thursday now. If she wanted to find anything out, she'd have to work fast. But no more signs were forthcoming. So she just sat and tried her next wine.

Eventually, she knew she was going to call attention to herself if she stayed any longer. The room was thinning out some. People tasting wine obviously kept on the move.

"Can anyone come to that memorial service?" she asked the nicest woman of the pourers. "I've read about Mr. Daninger and wouldn't mind paying my respects. He seemed like an amazing man."

"That doesn't even begin to cover it," the woman said. "We are all still in shock." She handed her a printed card with the service address and time. "Lisa, his daughter, had these printed up, since so many people were asking."

"Thanks. Maybe I'll see you there."

"You'll see everybody there. At least, they better be there. This whole valley owes a lot to Bob."

Ruby pulled out her last card to be able to sit a bit longer and said to the woman, "I like these so much that I will join your wine club."

The biggest pitch here and every winery, she gathered, was getting people to sign up for their wine club. It made sense. If you had enough people agreeing to have you send them two bottles a month, your winery would be secure. This would probably be even more important to the smaller wineries but the sell was just as hard here. Plus she liked Anita, this pourer, a little more than the others and wanted her to have the commission.

She filled out the card, but with Shelby's address. Shelby was her most wine-drinking friend, so she would receive two bottles out of the deal and then Ruby could cancel it.

As she finished and handed it and her credit card over to Anita, there was a ripple of displacement in the room. Someone special or important had just walked in. The pourers stood a bit straighter. Almost imperceptible, but Ruby caught it.

She turned to see a very handsome man walk in. "Who is that?" she asked Anita.

Anita said, "That's Tom. He's married to Lisa. He really runs the place."

Ruby could tell that Anita was held sway by Tom's charms. To make herself noticeable to him, Anita lifted her voice and called over to him instantly.

"Tom? Would you like to meet our latest wine club member?" She looked down at the card. "Ruby Tuesday?" She looked at her again and whispered as Tom finished up with one of the employees and headed over. "Is that for real?"

"Cross my heart and hope to die," Ruby said. "Would I kid about something like that?"

"Guess you wouldn't." Anita looked beyond Ruby, beaming.

From behind her, someone grabbed her shoulders and squeezed them, just like you would a breast. Ruby turned to meet Tom.

50

RUBY VIEWED THIS HANDSOME man but with a much different feeling than Anita obviously had upon seeing him. Ruby was in shock. Behind the leering smile was a vat of darkness. Ruby had often seen darkness in people and it always shocked her when she met it, face to face. Yet it was clear to her that she and Jessica were the only ones to see it in Tom, at least around these parts.

"Well now, this is just what I needed to start my day!" he said, with undisguised intent.

Four o'clock was the time and it was the start of his day? Run this place my ass, she thought. But her Spidey sense was now on full alert and she was in full alert work mode.

She turned to him and gave him her best shy yet a bit

flustered smile, indicating to him that his charm was working on her completely but she was trying to hide that fact.

He lapped it up. "A gorgeous woman, by herself, signing up to receive my wines?"

Ruby laughed a little and met his eyes, smiling slightly with invitation. But inwardly, her eyes were rolling. Did no one catch the sheer pomposity in that statement around here? *His* wines? Apparently no one did.

"Now, did you know that I offer a very special service?" He put his finger under her chin and lifted her face to to look at him, brushing his other fingers lightly against her throat. A rather nice move, she thought, if it wasn't coming from Godzilla and had some genuine feeling to back it up.

He looked up and grinned at Anita and the other pourers, to indicate that of course this was all in good fun and they grinned back. Then he was right back to being dead serious in his pursuing of her. He had not stopped touching her, a little here, a little there...

"For my very special customers—and beautiful as you are, you have already made the cut—I can personally deliver your wine." He leaned in a little closer. "Would you like to have me do that?"

So much for having to seduce him, Ruby harrumphed. But she knew exactly what was happening and held her own.

She smiled, seemingly breathless and overwhelmed by his attentions.

"I think that would be very intriguing. But I live in Wisconsin."

He laughed, already past undressing her in his mind and ready to do the deed. "Just my luck. All the good ones are married or out of state." He looked up and laughed. Two of his male minions laughed too, right on cue.

"Lovely to meet you."

"Ruby."

"Ruby. What a gem you are."

She did everything but blush. She wasn't good at blushing. Though she knew how to manipulate these situations as well or better than most men, she never got to the point where she could fake a blush.

And with that, Tom walked away. But Ruby knew better. He thought he was playing her by building suspense. But she knew that he was on fire now and wasn't a guy who knew how to leave a feeling like this alone or take "no" for an answer. She just had to wait for the next move.

When he was out of earshot, she said to Anita, "Boy, he's a charmer, huh?"

"Oh yeah. He talks a great game but he is happily married. So don't get your hopes up."

At that moment, Ruby saw Anita's whole story. She wanted this man so badly that she would have had his kids. But he had flirted with her and not followed through. Smart of him. It made Anita have to believe that he never did. Ruby already knew better.

She turned to Anita. "Say, is there a fun place to go around here at night? I'm only here for a couple of days and I wouldn't mind getting out, to see the spots. Anywhere you guys like to go?"

"Night life here is a little slow. There is a karaoke place that is only open Friday nights. It is a restaurant the rest of the time. All the Daningers love to go there, drink wine and sing."

Karaoke bar, she thought. Whew! That works for me! If they had all gathered Friday nights to play handball, she would have been shit out of luck.

"Does Tom go, too?" she asked.

"Nope, you're out of luck there. He doesn't sing or like to hear his wife singing either," she laughed. "He just goes in town, drinking with the boys, his workers. They can get pretty rowdy."

They can get pretty rowdy but more importantly, they cover for him, Ruby thought. But a plan was starting to shape up nicely. Karaoke. No Tom. Bingo. She got the name and address of the place and when it got started, around eight o'clock.

Just then, the hand was back, stroking her shoulder, moving

under her hair to her neck. Tom.

"Have you seen the whole place, Ruby? I'd love to give you a tour."

"That sounds great." She got up and left with him.

Here we go, she thought. Game on.

51

WHILE IN EARSHOT OF the other employees, Tom gave a pretty good semblance of a tour. His stentorious voice rang out as they walked. The employees no doubt could overhear him and would know that he was giving the standard talking points.

Then Tom gestured for Ruby to turn into a supply room. They were the only ones in it.

"Ruby, come over here. Right now. Stand in front of me." She walked slowly, keeping eye contact with him the whole time, daring him to keep going. Before seconds could pass, he was all over her like a cheap suit.

"You're driving me fucking crazy, you know that?" he breathed, his hands roaming all over her, grabbing her breasts and her ass.

"I don't know that...," she pretended to stammer.

"Of course you know that. Ooh, but you're a nasty little girl, aren't you? Can you feel that?" He took her hand and put it down on his erection. She gasped, to show how excited she was. But at the same time, she had to wonder. In real life, has that move ever really produced the reaction some men think it deserves?

"Keep touching it. That's all for you. And then some. You want it, don't you? Oh, you want it. You need it. Tell me you want it. You want my cock up inside you." He yanked her hair back, hard. "Tell me."

She didn't take her hand away, touching him intently but a little too lightly, just to make him crazy.

Back in another time, she might have relented, just for the fun of it. It had been a long time between fun times with bad boys. But this was a very bad boy and not in an entertaining way. Time to follow up on her objectives.

"I do. I want it...," she said breathlessly.

A knock came on the wall outside the room they were in. He jumped away from her. A man's voice said, "Tom? Sorry to bother you, but I need you to sign off on some stuff so we can ship it out before the end of the day."

Ruby thought it almost comical that this man was speaking from the hallway when there wasn't even a door to the room they were in! Why wouldn't he just walk a few more steps and ask him in person? Clearly, he was one of Tom's minions. Tom clearly did this exact tour often and this was the room where he brought women to clinch the deal. How revolting.

"I'll meet you out front in a minute," he said, and the footsteps—a little too loud to indicate the coast was clear—yuck!—indicated that the man was leaving.

Tom turned back and pressed his erection hard into her. "Now see what you've done? You've started something that you're going to have to finish. You're going to have to suck it and make it all better. You know that, don't you?"

"Yeah," she whispered, "I will make it better. You know I will. But not in the five minutes you've got."

He laughed, kissed her neck and pulled her hair, "Ooh, you are such a little whore, you know that? Where can I meet you? When?"

"I'm sure we'll meet. One of these nights in town. I'll find you."

And with that, she turned and left. I won't meet him for a couple of nights. Then I'll have him right where I want him.

The trick—the necessity—was that he couldn't find her before then. But she felt pretty confident. The only address he could look at was Shelby's and if he flew all the way there to find her, Shelby would most likely end up doing him and thanking her for it.

Driving her car away and shaking off what had just happened, she mused. All that sex and he didn't even try to kiss me. Now who's the whore?

52

_____

THERE WAS NOTHING RUBY wanted more right then than a cold shower but she had the feeling that it was too soon to go back to Shady Pines. So she went back to a small bookstore she had seen near the Community Center and bought a book.

She was between books at the moment. She had finished her last one on the plane out. As an avid reader, she needed something fast. She was very anxious to read a story that was different than the story she was currently living. Walter Mosley, her favorite writer, had a new one out, so life was good! Wait, a new one with Easy Rawlins? He killed him off in the last one, didn't he? Apparently not. Well, hallelujah, he was still alive! Characters that good don't come along all that often.

She kept wanting to call Daniel but had made herself a

promise not to. His goodness and love would make her doubt her willpower and she couldn't do that now. The pieces were falling into place and she had to see them through.

Walking from Readers', the bookstore, she went to a beautiful little restaurant called The Girl & the Fig for dinner. She got a table in the back and read. It was still early, so she had a nice talk with the waitress and had one of the best meals of her life, with a perfect half bottle of wine to go with it. She found herself wishing she could take every bite home and share it with Reardon. Reardon deserved this elegant meal. She resolved that when she got back, she would ask Riley what the best restaurant in Milwaukee was and then take Reardon there.

She stepped outside into a balmy breeze. Man, this was like no other small town she had ever been to—both sophisticated and elegant while being casual and approachable. Not a person or place in the whole town was snooty; yet, everything was done with courtesy and beauty. Wow.

Back on the road, she retraced her route to Napa. Driving in the Beemer, listening to her tunes full blast, she felt insanely exhilarated. This wasn't real life and she was glad of that. But it was an adventure! She both embraced it and knew she needed it. Rural, Wisconsin, plus adventures like this? Her world was on fire!

And even more importantly, it was on track.

53

BACK AT SHADY PINES, she met up with Margie and a new guest, who had just checked in, named Dora.

"Dora, the Explorer?" It was out of Ruby's mouth before she could catch it.

"Very funny," the woman said, sadly. She seemed to be sad anyway and this didn't help matters.

"Dora, I'm really sorry. I didn't think. My name is Ruby Tuesday. Take your best shot."

Dora smiled ruefully. "You've probably heard them all anyway."

"You're right about that."

"Well, goodnight," Dora said and turned up the stairs to her room.

"Seems a bit early for bed, even for me," Margie said to Ruby. They sat and talked. She saw Margie's cookbook open.

"What's for breakfast tomorrow?" she asked her.

"Cheese blintzes with lemon ricotta stuffing and fruit-infused cream on top," she said, excitedly.

"Wow, Margie! That sounds intense. Do you expect people to walk around and drink wine after that?"

Margie chuckled. "Well, I barely can! Oh I know what you're thinking. And you don't even know the half of it. I have a heart condition and I'm cooking with cream!

"But I'm all alone here, you know. My daughter lives in Portland with her kids. She has a husband who is away on business a lot. Plus, she has a business of her own. So I never see her.

"And you know? Food is my favorite thing. I started making breakfasts. Then they got more and more luxurious and everybody loved them, so that made me happy.

"It's what I do. And people come here for it, so...," she trailed off. She started to rise up and then sat back down, clearly exhausted.

"Well, I'm feeling a little indigestion so I think I'll hit the sack now," she said.

"Okay and thanks, Margie." She didn't know why she said that, truthfully.

Margie caught it and said, "Thanks for what?"

Ruby look deeply at her and answered with truth. "For your companionship and your big heart. For giving people what they want. I have known what it means to be lonely. Not now, but at other times in my life. And from someone who you just met, you have made me feel really welcome. You connect like that with all of your guests. It may not be family of a standard type, but I'm guessing you have an incredible effect on those who stay here. More than you know."

Margie winced from her indigestion. She saw Ruby's look of concern and shrugged it off. "Oh don't worry. This happens all the time. Wait until after the cheese blintzes!"

She started to walk but turned back. "Thank you dear. I heard what you said and I appreciate it."

"I meant it. Sleep well."

Once in her room, Ruby went over all the events that had transpired in a little under forty- eight hours.

First of all, she looked at the signs. Years ago, she had asked a world-class psychic that she admired, "How do you know which ones are the signs?" The psychic had laughed and said, "Well dearest, I think I'd assume they are all signs!"

She had never forgotten that. She had followed the signs that had taken her to Jessica's for all of that information. The winery had taken her to Tom. Bingo.

It was abundantly clear to her that Tom was either complicit in or knew the story of Bob's death. Even the heavy seduction meant next to nothing to him, she was sure. It was just how he operated. But she was also clear that it meant something to the unfolding truth.

He certainly knew he had a mountain of an empire to lose if the place was sold. But maybe, either way, Lisa would allow him to speak for both of them in the decision-making. She already allowed him to strut around and parade as if the place was his. He couldn't be getting away with all that posturing without Lisa's allowance of it, on some level.

If things kept on track, she would meet some of the siblings tomorrow at the karaoke bar. That might hopefully give her the next steps. If nothing else, she knew she would be here till the funeral on Sunday. If she didn't get more information by then, she could try again with Tom, but she knew that the time for talking with him would be very short!

As she reasoned through it, she realized that there was something else that she had the ability to change. She could show Lisa undeniable proof of what this man did and how he operated. Whatever was going to happen to the winery, all the good people who worked there needed Lisa to have her eyes opened.

Ruby knew exactly what needed to happen. She was the

exact one and in the exact right position to do this. She pulled out her cell phone and walked outside and away from the B&B.

Riley answered immediately. She told him what she wanted from him and arranged for it to happen on Sunday night. The family would have to maintain good form the night before the funeral, so that wasn't the time to do it. But once the service was over, that was a different story. She told Riley that the guy needed to be very discreet. Whoever he hired could decide where she should meet him Sunday morning.

"Ooh girl, you are mixing it up out there. Love it! You've already got a good story going, no question about it."

"You got that right. It's gonna be a honey."

They talked a bit more, then hung up. It was only then that she realized how late it was there, with the time difference. She had probably woken Riley up. But his excitement was all she needed to hear. And at least she had that part of her plan in place. If she could pull that off, maybe that was all that would be needed.

54

OUTSIDE ALREADY FROM THE call, Ruby turned to walk back to the house, but then didn't. She felt herself turning and starting to walk away. The night was beautiful and she was a deep lover of long walks. But instinctively, she knew that this walk was about something in particular.

Turning on a few more streets, she had wandered into a residential area. There were a few gaggles of kids: everything felt safe.

At that moment, a car "vroomed" by, making as much noise as they could. Several college guys were leaning out the windows and yelling at anyone who went by.

When they spotted Ruby, they wolf whistled, talked amongst themselves and then yelled, "Are you lost, bitch?" The car raced on, trailing the sound of them laughing, so happy with their previous repartee.

Ruby wasn't for a moment scared. Living in LA for any length of time made one instantly immune from pretend threats. But as she turned to walk back towards the house, it happened in one instant.

Her body, mind, soul and resolve all buckled.

"Am I lost?" she wondered out loud, in a whisper. "God, maybe I am! Am I totally bat shit? Out there where the buses don't run? That lost?"

In an instant, her will, her resolve and her faith left her.

She started wracking her brain, turning every sign and action over from the column marked "divinely guided" to the column marked "a crazy woman's imagination." So what had she really come up with? Seducing the easiest guy on the planet to seduce? Whoopee.

As she could feel all her actions turning into doubt and worse, turning in on her with ridicule, she steeled herself and pushed all thoughts from her mind, going to the only one who could help her.

"Okay Sam, I think you need to get here and explain this to me."

There was a bench in front of someone's yard and she sat on it. And waited. Sam didn't come.

What had she done? Why was she here? Who would believe that she had come because of a voice in her head?

She started to sense she was going even further down, energetically. That made her think of the talks she had had with Sam in the past. He had begun to tell her about energetic shifts and equations. He discussed emotions, physicality, any number of things in terms of energy and how to lift it higher.

That's it! she thought. Sam probably can't reach me if my energy is too far down! So she started to do the work of pulling herself back up. Maybe that was the way it was supposed to happen.

So she tried to look at the whole trajectory of the trip from a different angle. She tried to see it from Sam's observation point, wherever that was. And try as she might, she couldn't find anything out of place. It had unfolded before her. Granted, maybe she picked this B&B and wasn't led to it. Who knew? But the elements to move forward on her plan were working perfectly.

And after all, isn't it a total idiot who doubts a plan that is so obviously working?

"Not a total idiot," Sam intoned. *"That seems a bit harsh."*

"Sam!" She almost shouted from where she was sitting. It was too quiet to even attempt a loud whisper, so she held back. "You're here!"

"*I've always been here. You were right, by the way-good work. I couldn't communicate because your system was in a form of energetic lockdown of sorts.*"

"So you couldn't reach me," she said softly.

"*Nah, but I was here. Always around, Doll.*" he said, using his affectionate name for her.

"What was that? What happened?"

She felt Sam's hesitation. "*Not to worry. You need to know the reasons. But they will be better explained later, when you are home. They wouldn't serve you here.*"

Ruby got the distinct feeling that someone was pushing her off the bench. Was he...?

"*Now get up, put your Spidey sense back in high gear and go forth. Remember, you are being of use!*"

He said the last part like Jon Lovitz would play PT Barnum. It made her laugh, which was the point.

"Sam, you can push me around physically?" she asked with a smile.

"*Ha! Child's play!*"

And he was gone.

55

RUBY WALKED BACK INTO the house, stepping as quietly as possible. She was used to living with Frank, who was a light sleeper. She knew Margie was about his age and didn't want to take any chances.

Tiptoeing past the small hallway that led down to Margie's room, Ruby began up the old stairs. The first step, just like they always did in the movies, made a big involuntary squeak. She cursed inwardly and began to approach the second stair. That was when she heard it.

Scratching.

Margie's door was closed, but Riley was in there. Should she let him out? What if he ran away? Well, she had to do it. If he ran, she would try to keep up with him. Most likely, he hadn't done his business earlier and Margie hadn't known that.

Cautiously, she walked down the little hallway and opened the door.

There, on the ground with Riley watching over her, lay Margie. She was unconscious.

56

AT FIRST GLANCE, THE Queen of the Valley Hospital in Napa looked like any other hospital. Except for two things. First, the fact that Ruby was in it. Oh, and the giant statue of the Virgin Mary coming out of the building as you approached it.

"Hey Mary," Ruby whispered. "If you could help us out here, that would be great." It was her version of a prayer, but a prayer nonetheless.

She had driven behind the paramedics, parked and ran in. There was no point in telling the nurses that she was a family member of Margie's because they all knew Margie already. But they allowed her to hold Margie's hand whenever she was not in the way.

The doctor talked with her. Told her that it was a heart

attack. It looked like she would survive but it wasn't for sure yet.

"She's had incidents before this, but this outcome was the one we were dreading. It was a matter of time. Thank God you were there, young lady. She wouldn't have lived much longer."

Ruby stayed with her all night. Maybe it was because she was the one to have found her. Maybe it was that she didn't think anyone in that condition should be alone. Maybe, she wondered into the night, it was because she hadn't done it with her own family, sitting with her own parents. She didn't know and after a while, it ceased to matter.

She stayed. And she talked to Margie about all sorts of things. If it was true that one of the things that pulls you through is someone there talking with you, then Ruby was determined to do her best to make that happen here.

Finally, about four o'clock in the morning, the doctor told her that Margie had stabilized and would be sleeping very soundly for the next few hours.

Ruby went back to Shady Pines. No need to wait for a sign to tell her what to do next. She called Danielle, Margie's daughter on the phone. The number was on the wall next to Margie's personal phone, so that was an easy one to find.

"Danielle?" she asked the groggy voice.

"Who is this? Do you know that it is four o'clock in the morning?"

"Yes, I do know and I'm sorry to wake you up. My name is Ruby and I am here, staying at your mom's bed and breakfast."

"Hello Ruby," Danielle said cautiously, alert to the fact that something was awfully wrong.

"I think the direct way is the best. Your mother suffered a heart attack last night." She heard a gasp but no sound followed it, so she went on. "She is going to live. She is in the hospital, resting."

"Oh God, oh God, oh my God!" Danielle yelled and then started to cry.

"Can you come down?" Ruby looked up at the key rack to check her accuracy. She was right. "There are six people staying here, two couples, a woman and myself. Can you come?"

"Oh! Yes, yes. I'll be there. My husband has the kids for the weekend on a fishing trip. I need to get them back and I have to notify some people at work. Oh my God, poor Mom! What can I do?

"Okay," Danielle said, now more awake and organized. "I can get there in two days at most. Can you just close the place down for now? Maybe for the foreseeable future? No, you probably can't. Can you?"

Unlike Margie's poor muddled daughter, Ruby felt strangely lucid.

"Danielle, you are in shock. You shouldn't even try to make

decisions like that right now. Just get down here as soon as you can to be with your mother. In the meantime, I'll run it for you. I'll run it for Margie."

"Wait a minute. You'll run it? I don't even know you!"

Ruby laughed at the absurdity of it all. "I know you don't, but life is handing you a gift so I suggest you take me up on it! Besides, from what I can tell, I'm a pretty good deal. I know how to clean and make beds. I can make one dandy hospital corner! Sorry. Bad taste. And I know more than a little about making breakfast. I had planned to be here till Monday, so I'll take care of it till then. It's Friday morning so come when you can. By then, maybe I can consult the neighbors for more help down the line. Deal?"

"Deal. And thank you Ruby. That doesn't seem to be enough to say."

"Your mother is fighting for her life, Danielle. And she's lonely. She has been for quite a while now. You are just what she needs."

With that, Danielle began to wail out of sadness and guilt. Ruby listened for a bit and then hung up.

For the next two hours, she prepared breakfast. A country breakfast with eggs, bacon and toast. Then she made a cinnamon loaf, just in case someone came for that.

When the guests came down, she told them one by one

what had happened and that she would be taking care of them, if there was anything they wanted or needed.

At first suspicious, they melted over her cooking. And though they moaned over her cinnamon loaf, she could clearly see that they hadn't come for that. They didn't automatically expect the richer foods. That had been Margie's delusion all along.

That was good news. She felt sure that people like these would keep coming to Shady Pines, no matter what was on the menu.

57

WHEN EVERYONE HAD HAD their fill, Ruby asked them to leave their dishes. She would clean them later. She had found Riley's dog food and fed him, though he looked very lost. He kept going to the door every time a car passed, thinking Margie would be coming any minute. It broke Ruby's heart all over again.

She went to the hospital for a couple of hours and held Margie's hand, even in slumber. While she sat there, Ruby kept talking with her softly, in case she could hear. As she did that, Ruby's mind was reeling, continuing to sort. She asked for Sam's help but he didn't answer. She knew he was there and that this part was as he had told her. He needed her to live with the events without figuring them out. Part of the cosmic rules...

Was she really here, on this trip, for Margie? Looked like it.

She had always assumed it was for the murder. But she was no closer to finding out anything about that. At any rate, there was nothing more to do on that front till the karaoke night tonight.

Watch and listen. She would do what she could. She was doing what she could. She told Margie softly that she would be back soon, before returning to her temporary home.

When she opened the door, she heard a vacuum running. The dishes were all done and stacked by the sink. Puzzled, she went toward the sound and found Dora in one of the rooms, running the vacuum with gusto.

"Oh, I hope you don't mind," she said. "I always clean at home to get my head straight, so I thought, why not?"

Ruby was thrilled. "I'm right with you, sister! There have to be a lot of things in this place that Margie hasn't been able to do for a long time. Let's find 'em!"

While they worked, they talked. Dora lived in San Francisco. Finding new things to clean made them both a little breathless and giddy and Dora began to loosen up a bit. Hard work allowed personal information to be revealed much easier. It wasn't long before Ruby got the story out of why Dora was here.

Dora was convinced that her husband was cheating on her with his personal assistant, so she just packed up to get away. It turned out to be easier for Dora to tell Ruby about the affair, something she hadn't spoken about to a living soul, while cleaning toilets than if they had been seated and facing each other. Less easy would be Ruby's explanation of why she was here. But Dora's story won the day, to Ruby's relief.

What is it with these playboys and their wandering lust? Ruby thought. Dora had called her husband a playboy. And just the day before, Ruby was certainly being felt up by one! Why, especially when they had someone who loved them, did they feel the need to roam?

Then she felt a stab. If she had Daniel, what in fact was she doing?

That was a good question, she told herself. And one that she would have to look at when all of this was said and done.

No doubt about it, she was in the right place at the right time to learn. And there would obviously be more lessons on this trip than she had thought there would be.

58

AT EIGHT O'CLOCK THAT night, Ruby walked into the karaoke bar.

Though it was hardly that. It was a beautiful restaurant, with one of the side rooms used for karaoke only on that night. Though they kept the volume to a minimum, which Ruby always appreciated anyway, the singers could still be heard in the main dining room. Several times during the night, people would wander over during dinner if they liked the singer or if they just recognized someone they knew by their style.

It seemed pretty clear that the top echelon of the Valley's thirty-somethings liked this tradition and kept coming back for it. That was the only explanation for why the restaurant kept it going and why diners didn't complain.

Ruby had chosen her clothing carefully. She could ill afford starting another flirtation, or whatever you would call the thing with Tom. That could really mess up the works. She left her blonde hair down, with a sweet hair clip, in a loosely swept back kind of way. Her outfit assured people that her body was good but she wasn't advertising for anything. It seemed important to Ruby that she wasn't thought back on as loose or flirty in any way, in case her plan backfired.

As she walked in, a cute young girl was onstage singing a funny rendition of "You Go to My Head," the old jazz standard. She wasn't really any good, but her energy was infectious. She was having a ball, which was always fun to watch. As she finished, the crowd erupted with much more gusto than the act deserved. It told Ruby that the singer was important, in some other way, to this community.

"Way to go, Lisa!" someone yelled.

Ruby gulped. That was Lisa? She looked sixteen years old! And cute as a bug. A brainy cute redhead with energy to burn. Lisa came back and sat down with what had to be at least two of her brothers from the sheer family resemblance. Her flushed face matched her coloring from the sheer excitement of performing. Ruby took a seat on the other side of the aisle.

Clearly a ringleader, she shouted for someone else to go up. Several asked her to go again, but she said she wanted to wait a bit.

For a moment, Ruby sat absorbing Lisa's energy. She knew she liked her. She also knew without question that this woman sitting across from her had absolutely no idea who she was married to. Oh sure, he had sex with her. Unless Ruby was quite mistaken, he would have had sex with anything with movable parts! But Lisa was absolutely not Tom's type. He had married her for the opportunity. Ruby knew that. She was good at knowing stuff like that and there was absolutely no doubt in this case.

Tom had said and done all the right things with Lisa and she had fallen hard, letting herself be wrapped around his little finger, manipulated at will. To her, it was love. Lisa was clearly very bright, yet without any filters for this kind of love.

Worst of all, Ruby feared, would Lisa fare worse and worse because of this blind spot now that her dad was gone?

Back with her brothers, the mood was gloomy again. Ruby had to remember that they had lost their dad. She listened in to their conversation about the up and coming service.

"But she has a terrible, old person, wobbly voice and besides, she's a toad. I say we just don't have music at all," one of the brothers said.

"You have to have some kind of music," a nearby friend added.

"Yeah and I know the two songs that he would want," Lisa

said. "He loved 'Amazing Grace', of course, and his favorite…"

Without a pause, they all chimed in "Pennies From Heaven."

"Maybe we could all sing that one. Dad sang it enough," her brother mused. Though no one said anything and it was clear that no one found that idea plausible. Finally, Lisa spoke again.

"I agree that they wouldn't be good coming from the toad, but I don't know where else to turn. I think it's too rushed to find anybody else."

Ruby recognized their conversation as a sign. It was her cue. Time to get asked to this party, she thought. She had been browsing through the karaoke book for possible tunes to request. What would remind them of "Amazing Grace" without actually singing "Amazing Grace?"

"I wouldn't mind going next," she said quietly to the guy running the machine. This was a strange room for karaoke-far more people here to listen than to sing-so they were currently in a lull.

Lisa heard her and looked up. "Yeah!" She clapped loudly as Ruby moved forward, to signal everyone else to start clapping too. It was applause with utterly no expectation that she was going to be any good.

For the singer in Ruby, that kind of applause was her favorite kind. Its low expectation presented to her as a dare. The best kind of dare.

She would start the song quietly, to hook them in. She had chosen Whitney Houston's "I Will Always Love You." In point of fact, she hated this version, much preferring Dolly Parton's own simpler, more heartfelt recording. This one was soupy and over the top. But she hadn't had any more time and thought it could get the job done. Plus, Riley had confessed to her the night before she left that he loved soupy ballads, so this seemed even more right. She silently dedicated it to him.

Crossing past the expensive karaoke machine, she surreptitiously clicked a little knob on it twice. She had a good idea that the guy running it didn't even know the knob was there. But it took the song down two half steps, placing the modulation in the middle of the song, where it went up a step, right where it needed to be, to be in the biggest part of her voice. She knew her keys.

She started out a bit theatrically, singing the first verse very quietly and with almost a quaver in the opening notes. She sang the words with a vocal purity but without giving the listeners any sense of what would come next.

Up until that point, she had more or less lulled everyone into thinking that this was all she had in the tank. But then, just as Whitney had, she started to build. As she built, she could hear all the extra noise in the building start to quiet down. That was exactly as it should be. She was in the zone.

By the second verse, the noise in the kitchen had quieted down. People were wandering over and standing outside to listen.

For the big last third, she transformed into the diva that she had in her, knowing that it was just for an instant. And then, it all came back in and she sang the last line very, very quietly.

"I will always love—you."

She held the last note for several more seconds, to the very end and beyond, pulling it back and back and holding it steady.

The song ended. Again, just like it had at the gay bar, there was an instant of silence. Then the place erupted.

"ARE YOU KIDDING ME?" Lisa screamed. The whole place stood to applaud.

Man, Ruby thought, as she took a couple of bows and went humbly back to her seat. Guess I ought to do this more often.

She had hardly taken her seat when Lisa was right there.

"That was ass—ton—ish—ing."

Ruby gave her a warm smile. "You're very nice to say that."

"No, I'm not. I mean, I am nice. But this is a fact. You can sing!"

They smiled again.

"Go ahead," her brother yelled, "Ask her! We're all waiting!"

They spoke for about twenty minutes, each woman liking the other, each with a strong trust in their instincts. Lisa heard and felt what she wanted to hear and Ruby left, having agreed to sing both of Bob's favorite songs at his memorial service.

Happy to.

59

SATURDAY MORNING, RUBY AROSE to serve breakfast again to the Shady Pines boarders. About an hour or so after starting, Dora came downstairs and the two women fell in sync easily and wordlessly. They had formed an alliance, not so much as friends but as co-workers. Ruby knew Dora enjoyed the work and rising to the occasion as much as she did.

After everyone had been fed and the two women had finished the dishes, they decided to look at the backyard. It looked horribly neglected. As they puttered around, Dora made her first actual joke about her life since the two women had been here together.

"Man, about half the stuff we're doing, I need to do at my own house," she cracked.

Hardly a world-class wisecrack, but a joke nonetheless and a mention of something not altogether negative about her home, which just about had to be a step forward, Ruby thought.

It was while they were working in the yard, making a racket and pulling down dead branches, that the neighbors started coming by, one by one. They had heard the news that Margie was in the hospital in intensive care and wanted to know the details. They asked what they could do.

As Ruby spoke with them and explained the situation, she elicited two promises from each neighbor. One, that they would try to help keep the place going from Monday on, until Margie and Danielle could take stock and figure out how to proceed. The fact that none of them had ever even met Danielle made Ruby sad. She found herself sending out a hope to the Universe that Danielle might have the same sad realization when she got here.

The other promise concerned a happy change that the doctor had told her. Later this afternoon, a room was opening up that Margie could be moved into. She could have visitors in that room if they came in one at a time and didn't stay too long. She assured each neighbor that it would really mean a lot to Margie. They all seemed to be reassessing how they had treated Margie or hadn't treated her. Ruby sent up another hope that they were going to try to make it up to Margie. That alone would be amazingly healing for her, Ruby was sure.

Around one o'clock, Dora left to go out and see some sights. Ruby didn't join her, knowing that she would see enough sights tomorrow. She lent Dora her maps for the afternoon. The fact that Dora was going out on the town seemed really a positive step.

60

———

DORA HAD BARELY LEFT the driveway ten minutes earlier, when another car drove up and parked in the spot she had just vacated.

An older man got out. He walked with a little difficulty as he came toward the front door. He was sporting an old fashioned felt-brimmed hat with a feather in it, the kind her grandpa used to wear.

Ruby opened the door and stepped out to help him not miss the rather big step up. Several times already she had surmised that, were she drunk, she would have missed that danged step every time. So she helped the older man in. He turned to her at the door.

"Excuse me, Miss, but is Dora here?" he asked.

Nah. It couldn't be.

"You know, she's staying here but she isn't here at the moment. Was she expecting you?"

"Good heavens, no. I'm her husband."

This was the playboy? Wow. It took all kinds. "You know, she just left."

He shrugged. "I know. I saw her leave."

Now Ruby was lost. "But...?"

"You see...may we sit down?"

"Of course," she hurried to help him into a straight chair. If this guy was the fast mover that Dora had painted him to be, then she'd like to watch and time how fast those moves ended up happening. She might be able to take a nap in the time that experiment would take.

He was gruff and obviously completely unused to talking about private stuff to anyone much less Ruby, a total stranger. But he needed to talk. So, though both he and Dora were a bit on the cold side, Ruby softened to him and his predicament. She waited him out.

"The thing is, Miss...I'm just gonna say it. She thinks I'm having an affair with my secretary. Well, young lady, she has thought that with every secretary I've had, of which there have been the three of them. True, this one is a little easier on the eyes than the other two. But that's beside the point. When she accused me of having an affair with the first one, I would tell her to have her eyes checked. When she accused me of having an affair with the second one, I told her to have her head examined."

Could have been a funny line coming from someone else, Ruby thought, but not from this serious guy. It did seem like Dora was over the top with this, but he clearly didn't make things easier for her.

"Then, this little chickie baby I got now? I admit she is a looker. So what? She's easier to look at than number one was and a whole lot easier to look at than number two was.

"But she's half my age. I mean really. I'm gonna play hide the salami with a girl who doesn't even know who Benny Goodman is?" Ruby shrieked and then laughed out loud at that. How could you argue with that? It brought a little smile to his face.

"But anyway. Here she comes, giving me all this guff about the fact that I'm fooling around with this girl. And you know? I've now heard this forever. So I get sick of it, you know? Just sick of it! I'm hot under the collar now! So I say, 'that's for me to know and you to find out'."

"Uh-oh." Ruby said.

"Yeah, I know. I know! You even know! But you weren't around to stop me then, were you?" Ruby smiled. "Nope, sorry. I should have been there."

He looked at her, with a half smile. "Oh, you're a smart one aren't you. Well anyway, this tomato that works for me? Turns out she's a really good secretary. She cared that I couldn't see so well and that I wasn't up to date on the way to run certain things in the office..."

By that you probably mean everything in the office, Ruby thought. Wonder if he can even make his own coffee...

"So if we spent extra time, that was what it was on. I just didn't feel like having Dora haul that into the gutter like she always did, you know what I mean?"

"Yes. I do." She decided to be kind.

"Well, now I think I've blown it. She came here. Maybe she'll make good on her threats this time and leave me."

He sat for a while, then pulled a card out of his pocket.

"I wrote her a note, asking her to come home. She thinks I stink at writing so it might not even make a dent. But I thought, what the hell."

Under the crusty exterior, he was really hurting. For him anyway. She felt for him.

"I didn't want to run into her in case she started yelling at me again. So if you could do me a favor and slip this under her door tonight after she goes to sleep? She thinks better in the morning.

"I left it open. If you want to read it. Throw it out if you think it's awful."

He sat there for a moment. Only then did she realize that he was asking her to read it now. She read through it. He was right. It stunk. It wouldn't move me to walk across a room to you, she thought. Then she had an idea. She looked up at him.

"I'm sure she will appreciate that you came all the way up here to express this. I'll do as you say and slip it under her door. But let me ask you something. How do you really feel about her?"

He thought long and hard. But when the words came out, there was an urgency about them.

"I love her. I don't want to live without her. I'd be lost without her."

How interesting that was! The tone and the energy were all wrong. But the words were right. He had said he'd be lost with a tone that sounded like he needed her to make him some eggs. Yet, the words were the true thing here. Not said well. Perhaps never had been said well, but they were true for him. She knew what to do.

"Thank you for this. I'll pass it along."

"You think it'll be okay? Enough?"

"I think it might. I'll keep my fingers crossed for you."

"Thank you, young lady. Bye now."

And off the supposed playboy went, hobbling down the sidewalk to his car.

While they were still fresh in her head, she sat down and wrote a note to stick into the other note. She told Dora that she had seen her husband. She wrote his parting words down and framed them in such a way that they sounded ultimately romantic. If Dora really loved him, then this would probably give them a chance.

She tucked it away for later.

61

___

IT WASN'T FOUR O'CLOCK but more like five o'clock when Ruby got back to the hospital. She put a small bunch of flowers she had picked at the foot of the Virgin Mary, thanking her once again. Asking at the desk where Margie was now, she was directed to another part of the building. When she got there, the first neighbor that had dropped by earlier was waiting out in front of the room.

"Mr. Thornton, how nice to see you here!" she exclaimed.

He blushed a bit. "Well, you know, it's the right thing to do. Besides, we all love Margie, you know."

"Well, you are just wonderful to come. Who is in there now?"

"The doctor. He'll be out shortly. Do you want to go in first?"

"No way. I hate when people break into the line, don't you?"

She waited until the doctor came out and Mr. Thornton went in. As she waited, one and then another neighbor showed up, until there were four of them waiting in the hall with her.

Suffused with happiness at this turn of events, Ruby begged out of the picture, saying she would come back the next day. She left but not before doing one more thing. Seeing that an older neighbor lady had brought Margie some homemade fudge, she leaned down to her and said, without knowing the woman's name, "Would it be alright if I offered this wonderful fudge to the nursing staff instead?"

The woman's face blanched as she realized. "Oh my yes. That would be better."

With just a few hours left of the night before her big "mission" day, Ruby knew of one last little guy she could show some love to. She went back to Shady Pines and played ball with him in the backyard for a while.

Later that night, a bit restless, she turned on the television to see if she could be distracted. A loud commercial came on.

"...with it, you can hear conversations up to a mile away!"

She turned the channel to a mob show. A thug was patting another thug down.

"We have to pat you down for any listening devices, as you well know."

She turned it again. It was a show about Native Americans with a single recorder playing in the background. She turned the TV off.

"Okay, okay Sam, I get it!" she said out loud.

She called up Riley. "Apparently I need a recording or listening device from this guy too."

He made a horrible honking noise.

"What was that? A nasal problem with your latest dream date?"

"Nah, he'd be out of here if that was the case. I can't be bothered with that. No, you see, that was merely me making the deafening sound of a wild goose chase, for future reference."

"Wow. Oh ye of little faith," she said. Although as she said it, she realized that her lack of faith had vanished. Nothing was solved yet, but it was just so unimportant now that Margie was going to be all right. The rest could be examined later, if need be. For now, in for a penny, in for a pound, as her grandmother used to say.

"Okay honey. Marvin will have said recorder with him tomorrow morning."

"Marvin? His name is Marvin?"

"I know, I know. It's unfortunate. Maybe you should have called Central Casting. But I'm told he is a whiz with a camera. The best at getting 'the stuff', as they referred to it."

"Thanks. For doing this with me, Riley."

"Wouldn't miss it. And I won't miss it! Details, details. I have an inquiring mind and will require them all. Good night."

By this point, Riley the dog was hanging around with Ruby. She let him sleep on the bed with her, something she didn't think Margie did, but screw it.

Nodding off, she awoke with a start. "Shit! I almost forgot!"

Jumping out of bed, she went down the hall to Dora's door. From outside listening in, she could hear light snoring. Coast was clear.

She slipped the envelope with both notes in it under the door and went back to her room to sleep.

62

RUBY AWOKE, FEELING RESTED and ready for anything. And anything was what she knew she was going to get!

She went downstairs and made a big pot of raisin oatmeal with a sign that told everyone to help themselves. She didn't want to run into anyone this morning. Had to keep her head clear.

Back upstairs, she collected up two clothing changes, in addition to what she was wearing. It was imperative for her to look completely different in every part of the day and night.

Arriving at the square in Sonoma, she realized she might have gone a little overboard. Glancing at her reflection in a shop window, she was this woman standing in the midst of all these people who had dressed appropriately for the late summer months—women wearing summer frocks, Bermuda shorts on the men, etc. And there she was, wearing a sweatshirt with the hood up and jeans.

"I look like the Unibomber," she said aloud, to no one in particular. "Ruby, you're just meeting a PI, not the FBI, for God's sake."

"You'll get better at it as time goes by," Sam dropped in to tell her, with a wink in his voice. And just as quickly, he was gone.

"Oh swell. Now you drop in!" she yelled into the air. Passing tourists looked at her strangely and she realized she said that out loud! Well, she thought, at least she was ready for today.

She suddenly felt very strange. What was she doing here? But she argued, inwardly this time, that it had all led up to this.

In for a penny, in for a pound, she thought again as she neared the duck pond in the town square where the meeting with the PI had been arranged. Marvin. Her date with Marvin. Questioning things now would merit next to nothing.

She did believe in the information she was getting and while it could feel crazy-making at times, it also felt right more times than not.

Besides, hadn't she already been used in a perfect way to help out Margie? And if so, she couldn't see that she could screw this up too badly. Things were in motion and maybe they would come to nothing, but she felt certain that she could back out of hurting anybody, no matter what happened. Stop with all the probabilities, Ruby, she thought. She had put things in motion and had to do the best she could. Things would sort themselves out later.

She made it to the duck pond. Immediately a man walked right up to her. It must be him, she thought. Brazen the way he walked right up. Then she realized that the secret stuff hadn't started yet! Of course, he'd walk right up!

"Ms. Tuesday?" he said, with a tired but unmistakably British accent. "Is that what we are calling you?"

She had her first laugh of the day and it felt good. He thought Ruby Tuesday was a code name they were using!

"That's what we've been calling me since I got drunk in college and changed it legally," she quipped. Now he laughed.

"And that accent of yours is real as well?" she quipped.

"It would appear so. I can't seem to dodge it." With that, he smiled and then immediately dropped the smile. Like he'd had enough socializing and playtime was officially over.

He guided her to a bench and they sat as he went through the gizmos he had brought for her to use. Well, gizmos was her word for them, at any rate. Ruby had always loved gizmos. Gizmos had ushered in her lifelong devotion to James Bond. At this point, she was grateful to him for over explaining each gizmo to her like she was an idiot. In another situation, she would have bristled at it, but for now she was grateful. It was scary to think that she could screw the whole thing up on a technicality.

Marvin started with the recorder, describing its use. He asked where she wanted to wear it. She thought of later in the evening and wondered where Tom would not immediately paw her. They settled for her belly button. It was, thankfully, an incredibly tiny device. He gave her a leather wristband that had a switch to turn it on and off.

"But this will run for about six hours, so I'd leave it on from the beginning to the end, with the exception of when you are totally away from the action," he said.

She wasn't expecting the other gizmo he gave her. It was a little thingie, no bigger than a dot. He suggested she put it behind her ear, explaining that it was a small homing device.

"Why would I need that?" she asked.

Again, he was patient with her, seeing and sensing that she was nervous. His voice got lower and slower as he explained.

"Even though we will have a rendezvous point at the end, I need to know where you are at all times. Try to get out the back door of somewhere with the gentleman so I can get better pictures."

"Believe me, nothing about this thug is gentle," she said, relieved when he chuckled in response.

"That's why we're doing this. Don't forget that. You must keep your head."

To quell her doubts one more time and thinking of Lisa and how much she liked her, Ruby asked him, "You've been doing this a long time, right Marvin?"

"Long enough to get what you want."

"Oh no, I didn't mean that. My friend says you're the best so I have no doubt it's true. But what I want to ask you is...do you think it's always better if the spouse knows?"

He thought about that for a moment. "Yes. In cases like this. Yes. And remember, a lot of lives are affected if she doesn't know."

"You know, you're right!" Ruby said excitedly. "Thank you for saying that, Marvin. I was forgetting about that."

He pointed out his car and told her that he would be as near as he could when she was done.

"You'll find me and get the pictures, right?" She apparently needed one more reassurance.

He was the ultimate professional now. "You do what you're supposed to do and I'll do what I'm supposed to do. You're the rookie here. You can count on me."

And looking at him, she added one more thing. "Remember, if at all possible, not my face or hair. It's important that she gets that I could be anybody."

"Got it."

"Oh and Marvin? Are you going to be wearing that jacket?

You might stick out in an alley."

He looked straight at her and with the ultimate British deadpan said, "I change into my cat burglar outfit later."

She laughed. The meeting was over. And maybe, just for effect, he was instantly gone. She took a minute before looking around. She didn't see him anywhere. He had faded right into the crowd.

This guy was good. She was getting excited.

She had half an hour to kill before getting ready. Just fade into the scene, she thought. She stopped into a restaurant supply place to buy something for Reardon and her shop. All she could find was a joke gift of a collapsible whisk. At least she thought it was a joke. Who needs a collapsible whisk?

63

WHEN RUBY GOT TO the reception for Bob Daninger, she walked into the scene quietly. She didn't want to stick out too much and, especially, not too soon.

She had selected a dress from her old LA days. She had always liked it and, as dressing up goes, she felt comfortable in it. God knows, she didn't have much reason to wear it back in Rural. It was black and elegant, with two ivory striped panels that came down on either side, hugging her body. It didn't cut into her anywhere, which felt nice. She had taken the tiny mike out of her belly button for this portion of things and had put in on the outside, on her wrist. Marvin thought that made sense and had okayed it.

Ruby's first thought upon arriving was that she was a bit

overdressed. Her ponytail made things a little better, but these were people who worked crops after all. She loved that about them. They raised the most delightful bacchanalian crop ever. They had a very sophisticated earthy casualness about them. Not for the first time, she reflected that many of them would get along great with her friends back home in Wisconsin, talking soil and crops and the like. People weren't so different...

"Ruby!" Lisa yelled from across the field, as she started over to greet her. Ruby wondered if Lisa's big voice was to compensate for her little frame and young appearance. But whatever it was, she liked it.

"I'm so glad you are here! I was scared you wouldn't make it."

"I wouldn't have missed it for the world," she told Lisa. She meant it. "Your father was an amazing man."

"The best guy ever. Well, along with Tom of course. My husband." When she mentioned him, she blushed a little. It was clear she had complete blinders on where he was concerned.

Ruby felt like this was a sign as well. Seeing that Lisa's blinders were still holding, it made her even more determined. Still, as to the murder, she had to keep an open mind to anyone who might be involved in the bigger picture. She'd read enough mystery books to know that it was almost never who you thought it was.

The service was set up on a separate part of the estate, with the larger office rooms for the winery in the building behind the memorial set up. They had put up a stage of sorts, with several hundred white chairs in front. Clearly they were expecting quite a few people. This man was loved and deeply respected.

Ruby had a little psychic hit right then and asked Lisa if she could stand a bit away from everyone else on the dais.

Lisa looked at her strangely. "Of course. We're not formal here. But why?"

Ruby immediately reached for a false answer. "Because I didn't know him and you all did. It would feel false to me to be sitting among the family."

To her relief, Lisa was touched. "I get that. You're great, Ruby. I know you are leaving tomorrow, you said that, but let's keep in touch after this."

"I know where to reach you." Ruby felt a pang saying it. Lisa was a smart girl and, after tonight, there was a strong chance she would never want to speak to her again. It's so too bad if it had to end that way. She liked Lisa. Man, this espionage shit was hard!!!

Lisa left and was immediately absorbed into the growing crowd of people showing up. Lisa's brother that Ruby had met the other night, materialized by Ruby's side and handed her an envelope. "Here you go, Ruby. Thanks for doing this."

He left immediately. She opened the envelope to see three $100 bills inside. She opened her mouth to protest but there was no one there to protest to. Besides, it was good form to take it, even if they hadn't talked about money at all. She thought, well, I'll use it to get drunk on the plane. But wait! First class! It's all free!

Just to ground herself, Ruby took out a pen from her purse and wrote BARN FUND on the envelope.

64

———

THE CEREMONY FOR BOB had started. Many people sat and some stood around the edges of the seats. The family members were all on the dais, looking out. The group was crying at times and laughing at times as one by one, people stood and recollected great Bob stories.

Tom hadn't seen Ruby yet. That was her intention. Besides, he was busy working his flock. She could see a few women in the audience, staring at him with inappropriate sexuality coming off of them. He probably saw them as just a few regulars between his many conquests. She watched him smile at them, but not overtly so. He was good at this, she thought, with more than a little disgust. Like that old variety act on the Ed Sullivan show, Tom knew how to keep all his plates spinning in the air.

Lisa had gone over the order of the service with Ruby just before it started. She knew when each song should happen and "Amazing Grace" was up fairly early. Now was that time.

She stood. All eyes were on her. Tom saw her for the first time. He was slack jawed for only an instant, but she saw it. In a split second, his composure was back.

She closed her eyes and sang the song.

There was no applause. She hadn't wanted there to be. More people were crying though. This was right; as it should be.

Only a few moments later, she sang again. She started in a way that she knew would surprise some and confuse others, but both would know soon enough what she was singing. Starting in quietly and conversationally, she sang about a long time ago when no one appreciated the simple things.

People listened politely and looked up with different expressions, questioning where she was going with this. Ruby stole a glance over at Lisa, who was trying to figure out where she was going with this. But she was ready for them and continued. She sang of the reasons storms blew up and then came to the last line of this intro, concluding it with:

"Every time it rains, it rains pennies from heaven…"

At the mention of pennies from heaven, smiles lit up around the crowd. Huge smiles, as this was Bob's song. They mouthed the words for a minute and then grabbed the hand of the person they came with. A beautiful sunny energy came together. Ruby could see that this song was this man's signature. And boy, was he ever loved.

"They'll be pennies from heaven for you and for me."

This time there was applause. She nodded, ever so slightly, to acknowledge them and then took her seat.

There was, it looked to be, about twenty minutes left of the service. She was sitting and listening to each word when Sam came to her.

"Go to the bathroom," he said.

She didn't know how to do that. Just get up and leave? Thinking quickly, she realized that this must have been why she had gotten that hit that she should sit off to the side. But no one was moving. Just then there was a small sea change in the proceedings, with several people on the dais moving and someone else walking up.

"Now," Sam said softly, but as firmly as he had ever said anything to her.

She stood, a bit hunched over, and crept quickly down the stairs on her side of the dais. To her relief as she glanced back, no one was watching her.

She walked around the back, under the auspices of trying to find a bathroom. There were porta-potties out front, but with her straight, stretchy dress, any woman would have wanted a more sophisticated bathroom.

Walking around the side, she heard voices. Not wanting them to see her, she crouched down near a white table-clothed table. There were about two dozen of those white tables there, obviously waiting to be moved into the now chair-filled area for food directly after the service. But no one was back there now. She couldn't see the two men and their voices were rather quiet and low, but she and the gizmo could hear everything.

"Do you think they will still sell, now that the old man is gone?"

"Yeah, I do. Sad thing that. If Tom hadn't embezzled so much money out of the place, they'd be sitting pretty."

"How could everyone have missed it?"

"Have you seen their new accountant? Homely as the day is long. He services her; she services him."

"Are you serious?"

"As a heart attack."

"But wouldn't they find out sooner or later?"

"That's just it. He had it all wrapped up. Every month she put money into a bogus account that ended up in his personal account. She didn't even know what she was doing, till it was too late. Then she would have been cooked along with him. So it was locked in. The same person I heard this from said that the accountant finally confronted him about it. They both knew she was stuck and couldn't say anything, so just to show her, he had her raise his payment higher."

"If you knew this, then why didn't you tell anyone?"

"The whole place was in quicksand; going down the tubes. If I told, heads would roll but mine would, too. Shoot the messenger, you know?"

"You wouldn't want to tell Lisa?"

"Her least of all. I like her well enough, but it is her love life that has brought us all down."

"And if they had to sell?"

"Then it would all come out. Why do you think we're having this service today?"

And with that, they walked away.

Gotcha, you slimeball, Ruby thought.

65

STILL CROUCHED BEHIND THE table, Ruby thought quickly. Was the stuff she had enough? Did she even have to go through with the second part?

Then she thought of Mary Jo Buttafucco. In her case, in order to not have to see how badly she had misjudged her husband, Mary Jo had stayed with him, proclaiming his innocence, even after getting shot in the head by his lover!

Lisa hadn't seen all of Tom and who he was, but she knew. Ruby was sure of that. She knew and she was deeply damaged by it. She just hadn't let it rise to the surface yet. And if she needed to face it soon while trying to keep a brave face for the company? Who knew how she would handle it. Plus, she had the simplest and deepest reason not to face it. She loved this man.

Standing up again, Ruby knew she had to follow through with the plan. Tom had talked his way around the embezzlement thus far. He might be able to talk his way through to the other side of the sale. But it would be harder for him to pull it off if Lisa had proof. And it would be much harder if she had photos.

Ruby merged easily into the groups of people standing around after the ceremony. She greeted people, accepting congratulations on her singing, deflecting any more questions about her by quickly steering it to talk of Bob and how she wished she had gotten the chance to know him and then moving on to the next group.

She didn't want anyone to see her looking for Tom. But she knew that there was no question that he would find her, eventually.

And he did.

"Can I borrow our songbird for a minute please?" he said to her current cluster of people with a big smile.

Veering her slightly away from the people, he made a show of giving her a big friendly hug.

"You were so wonderful!" he said, a little too loudly, so the nearby people would hear his jovial intent.

Then leaning in close, he whispered, "Where the fuck have you been? I've been going out of my mind."

"I've been around."

"Well, where you haven't been is where you should be. Lying under me, taking care of my every need," he hissed.

"Hmm," she said, standing a bit further away but still whispering, so as to not draw attention. "Now you know I can't wait to take care of that. See you in town tonight. I'll find you."

"But I may need to...," he trailed off, gesturing to all the people here.

"I leave town tomorrow morning."

She knew this was a fishhook right into his gills. Sex with her and then she leaves town? She might as well have been a present, wearing a big bow. And nothing else.

"After nine. In town. Don't disappoint me."

"Oh, I never disappoint," she said flippantly, looking right into him and then, for just an instant, taking her gaze to his groin. Then she went to find Lisa, to give her a hug and leave.

Driving away, she couldn't help but feel a sense of peace coming over her. Tom thought she was playing right into his hands, though the truth was that he was playing right into hers. She laughed a little, quietly. All those bars she had been to in her life, those men, that banter...the key had always been to enjoy it but to stay well above and beyond it. It couldn't matter or it wouldn't be fun.

Well, it mattered this time. But all that training sure did come in handy!

66

TO USE UP SOME time till the evening, Ruby went back to see Jessica at her leather store to chat. She told her about the funeral and how she'd gotten invited, how it went, etc. She had the feeling that she could have told Jessica everything, but there just wasn't time enough to develop their connection. She regretted that.

Afterward, she went to a diner out of town. She brought the *Sun*, the local paper to read. She had given up on the Walter Mosley book for now. She loved his writing too much to not concentrate on every word of it. And it would be impossible to do that until her bigger, all encompassing, story was finished.

When the time was right, she changed her clothes. No one in the diner was paying attention to her, as it was almost nine o'clock. They were cleaning up and starting to close down.

She put on a one-piece dress, with a leather skirt attached to a black mesh top. The effect was very good. Plus it had the advantage of hiding the recording device in her navel. It wouldn't be discovered, no matter how much he groped her, till they were in bed together. And she had no intention of it going that far.

Last step, hair down. Yep. Party time! She was ready.

She drove into town, listening to the Mavericks with lead singer Raul Malo. He came through the record and lifted her spirits, as he always did. This was way harder than the gay bar "mission" had been, she reflected. The hardest thing with this was the hours in between. But she psyched herself into the right head space and parked the car.

In front of her, she saw Marvin's car. He wasn't in it.

That's as it should be, she thought. In order to not call attention to herself, she walked a bit unsteadily, like she had already had too much. That act would drop as soon as she entered a bar. First one. The El Dorado Kitchen, clearly the swankiest one of all. He wasn't there. Then again, he wouldn't be. Way too showy, it was a place to be seen! She craned her neck around for a couple of minutes, like she was looking for someone, then went back out.

The Swiss Hotel had a smaller, dark, English kind of bar. It was completely packed, so it took her a few minutes to weave through the packed-in revelers. He wasn't there. She moved on.

Finally, she walked into Steiner's. A grungier bar for younger kids and workers, this place clearly loved its community, but not without a controversial approach to good hygiene. This seemed like Tom's kind of place. There was a very loud band banging hard to the delight of the kids listening. But no Tom.

She was beginning to think that maybe this was all for naught and then she saw a sign for the Bistro. Walking in, this was a sleepier place. She walked through to the back bar. And there, with a few of his boys from work, was Tom.

Show time.

67

"WELL, IF IT ISN'T our little songbird from earlier! Out for a drink and dressed to kill!" Tom introduced his two friends, who immediately said they were just leaving. They knew the drill, finished their drinks rather quickly and left, saying politely that it was nice to meet her.

There was a jazz singer up in the front of the room with a trio backing her up. There was a small crowd gathered to watch her, yet from where Ruby was, she could barely hear her! The sound in this room is really bad for a singer, she thought, and then put that thought out of her head. She wasn't a singer tonight.

"What can I get you, lovely lady?" Tom continued in his stage voice. "A nice Chardonnay?"

The bartender piped in, "We're pouring Daninger Chard

tonight. Can't do better!" This had happened before. He knew the drill.

She smiled at them both. "I'll take a shot of Jack."

"Woah!" Tom said, smiling. "My kind of woman! I'll have one too!"

She kept smiling. Game on.

Drinking hers down in one pull, she asked for another.

A frown spread across Tom's face. He didn't want to have her go down before he got what he wanted out of her.

Seeing his worry, she teased and whispered, "Not used to women who can hold their liquor, Tom? Well I can. Join me. You said you would show me a good time on my last night here!"

And with that, she pretended to pout. She couldn't hate more the women who did that, but it worked like a charm on him. It figured.

"Well, you heard her," he said to the bartender. "It is up to you and I to show her a good time. You take care of the first part and I'll take care of the rest!"

She was nauseated for a minute. The whole town was in on this. Poor Lisa.

Focus Ruby.

They drank and listened to what little they could hear of the singer with that weird sound system. Tom chatted amiably with her for a little too long. Ruby held up her end of the conversation but started to wonder why he was taking so long to make more of a move. Had he spotted someone in the room and couldn't? Then she realized his move. Ego that he was, he wanted her to ask for it! Yes, that was it. She resolved to wait another five minutes and then make things happen.

At the end of five minutes, she glanced down at her watch and said, "Well, this has been a lot of fun, but I probably better head out. I've got an early plane to catch tomorrow."

Was that a smirk she saw in the corner of the bartender's mouth? She counted that as a small victory. The guy had no doubt watched this dance hundreds of times and it probably never went this way. Women who either wanted Tom or were interested in his position in town were seduced easily, leaning into him. He was flirting with them, he was a celebrity in this town, he was sexy as hell and he wanted them. What's not to get giddy about? Game, set, match.

Ruby had not so much as touched him in all that time. It was a chess game and he was about to lose.

"DON'T you go anywhere," he said, grabbing her wrist hard and yanking it down. The effect was that she lost her balance for a split second and fell into him. She saw undisguised raw need on his face.

"Now I gave up a party to be here," he whispered, "and a party is what I expect.

"We're just stepping out for a smoke," he said to the bartender and, still holding onto her wrist, they walked out the side door and into the night.

68

———————

THEY HAD STEPPED OUT from the restaurant into a little courtyard that opened up to several shops and a Mexican restaurant. All were closed for the night, but there were a few people standing outside, smoking.

He kept them walking until they went out the back to a gravel parking lot. No one was around. No one? She hoped there was at least one "someone" somewhere near by. She had to have faith.

He shoved her up against the wall. No one in the courtyard could see them.

He started to passionately kiss her. He was pressed so tightly against her that she began to mourn the obvious loss of this mesh dress just from the splinters. But there was no time to relocate. She kissed him back, being the aggressor at times and at times pulling sharply away until he moaned.

"What are you doing to me?" he growled.

"Nothing yet," she said, enjoying the game.

"Oh, yes, you are, you dirty little whore. You know exactly what you're doing, don't you?" His hands were everywhere. These would make some good shots.

"You're trying to make me crazy. And it's working. God, have I ever worked up a load to jam into you."

She almost laughed at that one. She realized that this was his route to anonymous sex, which is what he had with every woman. She didn't even have to be here! His imagination was now running the show. She toyed with the idea of not even saying anything else.

"You don't know what you're doing to me," she said. Ruby could talk as dirty as anyone. In fact she prided herself on it. But this time she had opted for a little stammering, like she was blown away by him.

"Oh yeah? Tell me. Tell me what you want me to do to you." Yeah, feed my imagination. It's all about me, he was meaning. But as he was preparing for her words, he reached up her skirt.

"No panties? My kind of woman. Ooh, you're ready for me, aren't you?" And with that, he raised her skirt and slapped her butt.

Just to see if it doused water on him at all, she asked, "But what about your wife?"

"Forget about her. She wouldn't know good sex if it hit her."

Lovely, Ruby thought. A complete asshole. Plus a new low in my sex life.

Now, against the wall, he lifted her skirt farther. With one hand on each butt cheek, he spanked her again, harder. Ruby knew they needed to end this now. If Marvin doesn't have the shots by now, it isn't gonna happen, she decided. And she also had all the sound from this encounter. Time to exit.

She moaned at the last spank and then laughed.

"Oh my God, you've got me so hot that I've got to pee! Don't move. I'm a really quick pee-er, I'll be right back." She touched his cock through his pants and he moaned again.

"You better hurry back. We need to go somewhere."

She turned back and started to kiss and lightly bite him. "Yeah? Well, we'll go there and then I'm gonna take you some more places," she said, rubbing his cock and kissing his ear. "After all, no use you calling me a whore unless I can prove it." He moaned in ecstasy. "Be right back."

She hurried back into the regular courtyard and was in luck. The bartender was away from his station so he wouldn't be able to see her. She walked straight down the corridor and out onto the street. Looking wildly for Marvin's car and on the verge of a bit of panic, she quickly found it and him.

69

IN THE CAR WITH Marvin, Ruby was crying a bit and shaking her head rapidly from side to side to ease the adrenaline. He sat beside her, very quietly. They were a mile away from the square now, so that she felt safe. She unzipped her dress in back and reached around for the device. If he saw anything, Marvin made no motion of any kind. He knew what she had just been through, she thought. More sadly, she realized that, with what he saw every day, nudity probably took on a whole different, sad dimension. After a while, he spoke.

"You did really good back there. You didn't lose your head."

"Thanks."

"Sure you don't want to go into the PI business?" he said, with a smile in his voice.

"No!" she said, sort of laughing and crying at the same time. "You got the pictures, right?"

"No worries, m'lady. It's all there."

They were silent for a bit. "You did a good thing back there. For everyone. Really. Guys like that need to be stopped."

"Yeah, they do," she said, starting to feel more like herself. "I know they do." She thought about it all for a minute and then continued.

"This empire is set to crumble anyway but, maybe, when she recovers, Lisa can do it on her terms. I pray she can catch him before he takes off with all of their money."

"Well, you just gave her the only chance she'll ever get of doing that."

Ruby heard that and nodded. She was calming down now. "Yeah. Maybe I did. Let's hope."

They waited a while and then Marvin walked back to the square to fetch her car and bring it back to her.

When they prepared to say goodbye, he went back over what she had wanted him to do tomorrow.

"Oh, one last thing, Marvin. I know you'll use whatever snippets of his dialogue you think right to use. But please cut out the thing he said about Lisa and sex."

"But..." He obviously thought that was important.

"I know. It's a bullseye for our purposes. But we have

enough. And she doesn't have to hear that. No woman should ever have to hear that."

Not used to sharing his opinions in these matters, Marvin's droopy face softened. "I think I agree with you."

They stood and shook hands. It seemed odd to Ruby for the two of them to just shake hands, after what they'd just been through together.

Ruby was always personal with people. But this, she realized, was just business.

"Thank you Marvin."

"Anytime, Miss. You get some rest now. Oh, and Miss?"

"Yes?" she turned back.

"I can travel for work, if you need anything."

She smiled at him. "Thanks Marvin. Believe me, I'll remember that."

70

MONDAY MORNING, RUBY AWOKE and went downstairs to make breakfast for the residents of Shady Pines one last time. About thirty minutes later, Dora came in and started to help. Ruby needed the help, as she had planned an elaborate breakfast with savory and sweet elements. But not because anyone had asked for it. She just felt like doing it.

They worked alongside each other with minimal early morning conversation till Dora spoke.

"So you're leaving today, huh?"

"Yep. I'm leaving in a few hours. I'll tell you what, though, I won't soon forget my stay!"

They chuckled about that. "Well, I'm leaving too," Dora said, quietly.

"Oh?"

"I'm going back home."

"I'm so glad Dora. That's really great news."

"Thought I'd better get back there—do some of the stuff on my house that you taught me before I forget it."

They kept working.

"Thank you for what you said in that letter, Ruby. That really clinched it for me."

Ruby silently thanked Sam for the opportunity.

There was something else that Dora was struggling to say. Ruby waited her out.

"Ruby, when you saw him...how did he seem to you?"

She thought about her answer before responding.

"He seemed like a man in love, Dora. In love with you."

Just then, the front door opened and a woman came inside. She seemed like she was peering around, unfamiliar with the surroundings. Once she looked at the two women, though, she was a dead ringer for a younger version of Margie.

"Danielle?" Ruby asked, with delight. "Is it you? I'm so glad you made it!"

A world of emotions crossed over Danielle's face after they hugged. "It's about time, isn't it? About time."

Dora kindly added, "Well, you're here now!"

71

THE TWO WOMEN PLUNKED Danielle down in a cozy chair while they finished breakfast. They introduced her to Riley and filled her in on the neighbors and how they were poised to help.

After breakfast, Ruby said goodbye to Dora and went to the hospital for one last stop with Danielle to say her final goodbyes to Margie.

She went in first, hugged her and said goodbye. Then as she turned to leave, she said, "Oh yeah. I almost forgot. I have a surprise for you." She opened the door and Danielle walked in. Margie's eyes flooded with tears and then Danielle's did too. She took Margie's hand and they just cried.

"I've missed you, Mom."

"I've missed you too, honey."

After a few minutes, Ruby felt it was time to go. She started to slip out the door, but Danielle called out.

"Ruby, don't go yet!" She turned back to her mother and said, "I'll be right back, Mom. I'm here for a while."

She followed Ruby out into the hall, taking an envelope out of her purse, obviously with money in it.

"No," Ruby protested. "It's really okay."

"Yes, it is okay, so take it," Danielle insisted. "This is a token. I've had a good year.

"But more than that, more than mere thanks, you changed my life, Ruby."

Ruby understood, but knew Danielle had to say it.

"You stopped your life to take care of my mother and her business. I figured that if you, a total stranger to her, would do that, then I have to do it too.

"I've promoted my next in line at work to give her more responsibility. She's earned it. I am changing my life from here on. It only takes minutes to get here from Portland. And to think," she was starting to sob now, "that I almost lost my mother! I mean, she's my mother! What job could be more important than that?"

Ruby gently massaged Danielle's back as she continued. "I'm going to commute and bring the kids down and when Mom's ready, she can make the choice of whether she wants to stay here or come up with us. But it will be her choice.

"We have choices now. Because of you Ruby! Because of you, I didn't lose my mother! How can I ever...thank you?"

"You already have, Danielle. How could you thank me more than what you just said?"

They hugged again. "Take good care of each other," Ruby said and left, humbled by the very sweetest part of this adventure.

72

THE PLANE CLIMBED HIGH into the air as Ruby leaned back in her cushy seat. Man, this First Class is the bomb, she thought.

Bill Withers' song "Lovely Day" was currently playing in her mental loop. She loved the song and it often accompanied her mentally when she was traveling or happy or both.

The flight attendant came over with another First Class exclusive—a menu with three choices of entries, steak to pasta to salmon. They all sounded really good and probably would be! Oh, plus a whole wine list.

She looked at the wine list and started to laugh. The shocked stares from the other passengers indicated that laughing was clearly something First Class passengers just didn't do.

"Miss?" the flight attendant interrupted Ruby's thoughts.

"I think I'll finally try the Daninger Chardonnay," she said.

"Excellent choice," the flight attendant said. "People say it is very good."

"Yes, I've heard that too," Ruby said, her smile spreading. She twirled her right index finger in a circle. "And keep 'em coming!"

73

——

WHILE RUBY WAS IN the air, laughing and swilling Daninger Chardonnay, Marvin arrived at the Daninger Winery. He walked into their headquarters next to the sight of the service less than twenty-four hours ago. He carried with him an envelope that contained the audio of the two men talking about her father and the business during the memorial, several audio clips of Tom talking in the seduction, and a set of pictures that said it all.

He had something for Lisa, Marvin said. The secretary tried to take it from him, but he told her that Lisa had to sign for it. As she ushered him into Lisa's office, he turned the envelope right side up to show what he had written on it, FOR YOUR EYES ONLY.

As he approached her desk, he turned back to the secretary to indicate that she should leave.

"It's fine," Lisa said to her secretary, who walked out and closed the door behind her. "What can I do for you?"

He put the envelope on her desk. She saw the message on it and felt a little confusion. As he had often observed in the past, Marvin thought he could detect the initial gnawing of realization growing in the pit of her stomach.

"The contents of this envelope were compiled and paid for by someone who really cares about you. She says to please tell you she is sorry for your losses."

"Losses?" Lisa questioned the plurality in that statement.

Marvin quietly put one more page on top of the envelope. In Ruby's own handwriting, she read.

Lisa—

Please don't turn away from this. I am your friend. And the woman in this picture is one of many. Believe me. Ask around. Listen. And take your life back. I'm so sorry.

Lisa looked scared. With shaky hands she started to open the envelope. She looked up at Marvin. But he had already slipped out of the room.

74

IT SEEMED INCREDIBLE TO Ruby that on that very same night, she was in Milwaukee, sitting on the big couch with Riley and Shelby, telling them the whole Sonoma story, from start to finish. They hung on every word. After she finished, they collapsed back and digested it all.

Finally, Riley spoke. "Well Marvin came through like a champ. By the way, he sent me an identical set of what he gave Lisa."

"Should I look at it?" Ruby asked, nervously.

"Don't know. I haven't looked at it yet. Most likely won't but wanted to hear from you first. Anyway, I'll give it to you in about three months."

"If then," she said.

"Tell me, Ruby," Shelby said. "I don't mean to be crass…"

"Yeah, but you will be anyway." Riley chided her.

"Weren't you the least bit curious to see that thing through with Tom? I mean, I've seen you at a bar when you dallied with someone much less interesting than that. And he, to use your phrase, obviously has some skills. Was it Daniel? Are you all in with that one?"

Ruby thought for a time. She wanted to answer it right. "Tom did have a lot of skills. But he was a bad man. Those guys we met in the bars were just good-looking and stupid."

Riley gave a theatrical sigh. "Ah, my favorite kind."

"I do have a good man. If I put that kind of bad juice into the middle of that equation.it wouldn't have been worth it. I got all the juice at home I need with the swimmer. Plus, lucky for him, I've amassed some rather heavy duty unrequited juice to give him in the near future that I believe he will benefit quite a bit from."

"Best believe that," Riley muttered, with a wry look on his face.

She thought some more. "I did what I needed to do. The rest would have been gratuitous at best."

Riley shook his head slowly and looked over at Shelby. "Look Shell! Our little girl is all grown up!" He pretended to sniffle. "Her whoring days are over!"

"Hey, don't sell me short!" Ruby said, throwing a pillow at

him. "I ain't dead yet!" They all laughed.

On the way out the door to stay the night at Shelby's place, she remembered something, turning to Riley. "I have money for you."

She pulled out the envelope with $3,300 in it—$300 from Lisa for the wedding and also $3,000 from Danielle.

"No good, sister. We made a deal, remember?" he said with warmth. "I got my money's worth.

"What's this?" he said. He turned it over to see that she had written BARN FUND on it.

"Well there now, you see? You've made my aging gay man's dreams come true. Contributing to a barn fund."

She hugged him. "I'll name my first cow after you."

He shrugged.

"First the dog, now a cow. My cup runneth over."

75

DRIVING THE NEXT DAY to her real home, Ruby was bubbling over to talk with Sam.

"Oh my God, that was amazing, Sam! It was amazing. It was great."

"You did good, Ruby. Really good."

This was high praise coming from him.

To go somewhere and immerse yourself in a whole other culture...to stay open but solve things, follow hunches.

"It wasn't exactly as haphazard as you portray it, but I can see how it must have felt that way." She could feel him smiling at that.

"You were brave, Ruby. I helped you more in some things than you thought and less in others than you thought. But your bravery knocked me out."

"Kind of fun to know you can knock out a spirit, you know? But you nailed the word-bravery. That's it. You know, Sam, I think about my life and the only missing piece was something I found in myself in the middle of that trip. And it also brought back something that used to be my modus operandi.

"Moving back here, I have found love. All kinds of love. Love I could only dream of before I got here. From Daniel but also from Reardon, Frank, Riley, Shelby...and I feel roots. I think I feel them for the first time ever. I don't ever want to give them up.

"But while I was out on this...trip, I could be involved and not involved at the same time. Growing up, that was the very strategy I used to survive. But now, I can revel in it! I can go right to the brink and know that I'm not going to go over it. I can always pull back. That makes coming home all the sweeter."

A while later, she shook her head. "Wow. If that wasn't a wild ride, I don't know what is."

She drove along in silence, just going back through all of it. Then Sam was back.

"Think you'd be up for another one?" he quietly asked.

"HAH!" she screamed. "I have to sleep and laze around for about a century."

"Naturally," he said.

"But maybe...," she couldn't resist adding, "right after that?"

76

ON THE WAY HOME, Ruby had the urge to see Reardon. She knew that, in contrast with her Milwaukee total reenactment, Reardon wouldn't ask her for any details. She would just welcome her back.

She was right.

Reardon saw her coming in through the kitchen window and ran out to hug her. They both cried a little. Ruby couldn't believe how much she had missed being here.

"Gimme something hugely decadent!" she commanded.

Reardon shrugged nonchalantly and disappeared. She came back in with that original lemon pie that had started it all. There was a candle in the middle of it. She had made it to celebrate her friend coming home.

"OH. MY. GOD!' Ruby screamed. "I might have to marry this pie!"

"If you did, you'd be cheating on it with everything else we make," Reardon said, making a stab at a joke.

"You got that right!" Ruby winked at her, starting right in on the pie.

"So, anything new while I was away?" she asked, just to fill the space while she was eating and Reardon was watching her. She knew things didn't change much around here. And that was just fine with her.

"Well actually, there are two little updates to tell you about," Reardon said, speaking quietly.

Ruby paused, looking up with a mouth stuffed with pie.

"First of all, I heard from Claire. You remember Claire?"

"Of course, I remember Claire! How is she?"

"Well, when she found out you weren't here, she was reluctant to talk on the phone. She said she would come and see us soon. She would like to take you up on suggesting some woodworking classes."

"Fantastic!"

"And she said she had moved on from Laurel. They both agreed it was time to go their separate ways."

"Cowabunga," Ruby said, smiling with her mouth full. She didn't stop eating, just held up the hand without a fork in it and

Reardon slapped it with a high five.

Then Reardon sat down, across from her. Uh- oh. Was something serious?

Reardon told her that she had gone back to that bar in Madison. But this time, she had met a woman. They were going to meet for a drink. Ruby's eyes, above her pie-filled mouth, started to bug out. Reardon rushed to reassure her.

"Now, it's nothing much. I mean, I just met her and all."

Ruby sat back, digesting the only news that could have made her stop eating that pie.

"Buddy, this is the greatest news ever. I am so excited for you!"

"It may not be anything."

"Well, first of all, it is indeed something! And even if she doesn't turn out to be something, the ball is rolling towards something. This is just great." And with that, she had to have another bite of pie.

"Do you like her?"

"I barely know her."

"But you liked her well enough to say yes."

Reardon looked really embarrassed, but she was also starting to have fun. "I guess I liked her well enough to suggest it."

"SHUT UP!" Ruby jumped up and did a happy dance.

She sat down. "Can I take this pie home with me?"

"If it'll make it there, being alone in the car with you."

"Oh buddy! Now you're even telling jokes! Man, this is great."

They sat and looked at each other. Reardon spoke next. "Any tips for me?"

Ruby looked down at the pie. "Yeah. Bring her one of these lemon pies and you can name your terms."

"That good?"

"Well, it made at least one other girl we both know commit to slaving like a dog for you for the rest of her natural life!"

"You're right. I'll bring one."

77

RUBY WALKED INTO THE house. Frank and Mutt rushed to meet her. She couldn't have been happier to see them both. Mutt almost knocked her down. She managed to hug Frank somewhere in there, but Mutt wasn't having it. He had missed her too much. So she sat on the floor and hugged and kissed him till he could settle down.

Frank stood and watched the happy reunion and then gave her the sweetest gift of all with what he said next.

"My friend, this house was not the same without you."

78

———

SHE WASN'T EXPECTING DANIEL till dinner, but apparently he had made Frank promise to call him.

She was in the yard and he burst through the back door to greet her.

If Ruby wondered how she was going to feel about Daniel after her trip, she wondered no more. He took her face in his big, rough hands and kissed her, with all the love in the world. Then he hugged her, picking her up and spinning her around and around.

There was nothing better than what she had right here, right now, in this moment.

Well, almost nothing. She did have one little itch left to scratch.

When he put her down, she cocked her head and said,

"Once more unto the breach, dear friends?"

"Let's close up that damned wall. The English dead thought you would never ask."

Laughing their heads off, they ran upstairs together.

WANT MORE RUBY?

IF IT'S TUESDAY, THIS MUST BE AMSTERDAM!

Watch as Ruby is propelled into her second adventure! Involved with missing persons, performing live and a love triangle like none other.

It all happens in the SECOND RUBY BOOK...

TUESDAYS IN AMSTERDAM!

DUE OUT SHORTLY!!!

A word about talking with Spirit....

Nothing about reading Ruby is meant to change or convert anyone's viewpoint with regards to spirituality. Convincing is an energy that I personally hate. Karmically, it is the worst as well!

However, the book does reflect my experience. I talk with Spirit, openly and deeply, in different forms, every single day.

In this writer's humble view, the mindset that we could live on this planet, crawling around on it like ants on a picnic blanket, with no set direction, answers or perspective, in this vast creational Universe and yet somehow believe that we are all the life, love, spirit, animation and creativity that there is—is just shortsighted.

I don't base this on my beliefs. I base it on personal experience and truth. For those of you who sense that their experience synches up with what I'm saying but don't know where to begin the dialogue, begin talking with your higher self. It can connect you with all there is.

Be patient. Be open. And allow. Spirit is talking with us every single second. All we have to learn to do is listen. I find

Spirit holds answers and comfort that is as ultimately practical and grounding as it is lifting and expansive.

For those who, like Riley, think it's all hooey but liked Ruby anyway, glad you're here as well. Welcome! I appreciate all of you.

Cynthia

Acknowledgments

There are a lot of people to thank for the origination and completion of this book and its subsequent series. To date, there are four more Ruby adventures where this leaves off-coming soon!

First to last and everywhere in between, I am indebted to Cliff, my husband, for supporting me and always encouraging me. To be married to a fellow artist means that support for creation in one another is a bylaw! Thank God. But beyond that, even when money was tight, Cliff urged me to go away for a week a year to write. And perhaps the most astounding thanks to him-for not only accepting the spiritual material I was getting, but for being there at the lectures, taping them and asking questions! Can you imagine? There would be no flights for Ruby without the rich soil that is Cliff.

My first Ruby readers—Cliff Hugo, Micaelia Randolph, Lucy Hamlyn, Jessica Terwilliger, David Barker, Patty McDonough, Nancy King, Merritt Booster, Taylor Macrae and Pat Reed. I gave it to you for feedback and encouragement and you did that and more. A special thanks to Lucy for our call right when I finished this book that I will always treasure.

A deeply felt thanks to two friends and published novelists, Harley Jane Kozak & Emma Cline. Despite their brilliance and busy lives, they both took large amounts of time to go over my book and its direction with me. I'm very grateful and in awe of both of you and your talents.

Micaelia, I could start thanking you and never stop. But specifically, thanks for our weekend, where you helped me set up the process that is now this book. And what Micaelia started, it was you, Patty, that made me finish! You kept at me and helped me to face myself; to hesitantly learn the language of publishing. If there was a checkered flag lap of this publishing trek, it belongs to Patty. If people have this book in their hands, it is thanks in large part to you.

To Audrey Simmons, the true spiritual heavyweight, for creating a safe zone to connect with Spirit. You are a wise and deeply important witness to the worlds within the Universe. I salute you for your indomitable spirit and your sheer guts and bravery.

To my USC English 101 professor, who gave me an A+ on everything I brought in for the whole semester. Hard to imagine someone liking everything I write, but he did and it gave me a cosmic thumbs up. Can't even remember your name, but I'll never forget you!

My thanks to Mark Peterson, for talking with me about

woodworking and the love of tools, and to Tami Montoya, for consulting with me on fighting skills.

A heartfelt thanks to the community of Sonoma, that wrapped this world weary girl with love, friendship and support beyond her wildest dreams.

To David Barker, who created my beautiful book cover. Though I couldn't seem to disabuse him of the belief that the central theme of this book was breaking a lesbian's arm, we had great discussions about the cover that really helped me shape what I wanted. I am really grateful for your artistry, David. Your cover consistently makes me smile!

To my family, nothing like the Barnetts! We were four completely independent, strident, creative souls. Our unstated but collective resolve as a family of artists eventually created a safe space for me to stand by who I've become.

Especially to my Dad who never stopped seeking out the truth with the wisdom, compassion and humility needed to actually find it. I miss you. Every day, I am conscious of our shared traits. In another generation, we could have been friends, egging each other on to be brave. Maybe we were. Maybe we will be.

Any artist is fed and nourished by all other artists. It can not be otherwise. A huge thank you to all the singers who taught me how to sing, believe and communicate the truth, to my students who walk in and move personal mountains, to writers that give me pacing and luxurious storytelling, who enable me every day to leave my life, open their book and sit in their creative worlds.

And the art supporters! Can't forget them! To all the people who have come to my shows over the decades. I think listening is harder than singing!

Over to the non-physical...The first co-writer of this book was and still is Shivers, my Sam, who then assembled an amazing spiritual writing team, who have helped me to write books that I haven't remotely imagined till I started writing them. More on all of them and this process at a different time and venue.

This is the first Ruby book. I hope you like it! And if you do, there are four more in the pipeline and hopefully more after that. So my final and deep thanks go to you, sweet reader. For you to have read this is the highest gift you could give me. Hope you had fun!

Cynthia

Note: Despite my copyright page disclaimer, there is one real person in the book. Jessica does exist and owns a leather shop in Sonoma. Go see her sometime!

About the Author

Hmm. Cynthia Tarr. What can you say about her? [What should you say?!] She grew up in Appleton, Wisconsin, and Washington D.C., then graduated with a BFA from USC in Los Angeles, where she pursued a career in the arts until she didn't.

[I know what you're thinking. Is she a lot like Ruby? Well sure. If she was half her age with a perfect body, a penchant for cleaning and a toleration for early mornings, it would be like looking in a mirror. But they did meet once, in the hall of the Community Center in Sonoma, where Cynthia is the musical director and teaches voice. Yep, that was her. Anyway. Back to the author notes.]

A professional singer and songwriter, she has collaborated with Keb'Mo', Dori Caymmi and many others. Her husband, Cliff Hugo, is a bass player. [And a really good one at that!] They moved to Sonoma fourteen years ago and live there blissfully with their dog, Poppy. It was there that she finally recorded her CD, "Here's to Life." [available through her website and individually on itunes.]

Ruby is her first novel.

P.S. Oh, hang on. Almost forgot. She owns one share of the Green Bay Packers. Couldn't leave without saying that.

SPECIAL AUTHOR'S NOTE: You might have noticed that the picture of me is perhaps a teense young. But hey. It's my favorite picture of me. I will continue to grow older as Ruby's adventures continue.

Thoughts from initial readers

"Ruby is my new favorite character and I can't wait to read more about her adventures, her friends and her!"

"This book has everything: love, romance, adventure, spirit guides, sex, baked goods and wine! I picked it up at 9 p.m. and didn't put it down until I finished it."

"Without one extra word in the whole book, this story reads like a dream."

"At first, when Ruby came to Wisconsin, I didn't know what to think. But the people around her got incredibly likeable. And then, when the adventure to Sonoma started, the pace picked up and I was hooked. Ruby, wherever you're going next, I'll be along for the ride!"

One last note from the author...

Hi Everyone—

I'm going to tell you a little story and you come in at the end, so stay tuned!

Did you guys see the PBS Greatest Reads contest a couple of years ago? Well, I loved it. They canvassed the country, asking for people's favorite reads and compiled a list of the 100 top choices. Then you had that summer to vote for your favorites, every day if you so desired. I had about eight books on that list that I voted for whenever I could.

The day arrived in the fall when PBS listed the final order. As I watched it, I couldn't help but reflect on what a great list it was! Written by and centering around both genders, multiethnic, written for different aged readers old and young, book lengths that were both long & short...It was "all styles all the time!" as a drummer friend of mine once laughingly wrote on his business card.

I decided to read those hundred books in the decade of my 60s. I started two years ago and have read twenty of them since, as well as writing about my experiences of reading them in a blog. Should you have an interest in seeing them, I invite you to log on. The address is:

http://100booksin10years.com/

Just paste that into your address heading and you'll be there! And what I would really recommend is to join the mailing list, located towards the bottom of the first page. The reason to do that is that I post fairly infrequently! This way, though you are obligated to nothing, no cost, no nothing, you will get an email whenever I get around to posting my next book review.

Hope to see you there!

Cynthia Tarr

P.S. And write your thoughts to me there as well! Look forward to hearing from you.